THE SPARE WHO BECAME THE HEIR AND OTHER STORIES

THE SPARE WHO BECAME THE HEIR AND OTHER STORIES

THE EARLY ADVENTURES OF THE HEAD, THE HEART, AND THE HEIR

ALICE HANOV

Gryphon Press

Published by Gryphon Press
Waterloo, Ontario

Third Edition

Paperback: 978-1-7780476-4-0
Hardcover: 978-1-7780476-5-7
Ebook: 978-1-7780476-3-3

Edited by Intrepid Literary
Cover design by The Book Designers

TORIAN
N
W E
S
OREEAN SEA
FORBIDDEN LANDS
KINGDOM OF BETRUGER
MOORLOC'S CASTLE
DARREN RIVER
OGRE MOUNTAINS
VERLASSEN CASTLE
KINGDOM OF DATTEN
DARK FOREST
DARK FOREST
KINGDOM OF WARREN
OREEAN SEA
HESSEN
TACITA'S PEAKS
DARREN
OREANE
SOUTHERN KINGDOMS
FANS
MADRAS
BEAREN

Forbidden Lands
Salem
Cassandra
Tiere
Merlin
Ares
Celtics
Mire
Hades
Mystics
Poseidon
N

CONTENTS

BECOMING A RETURNED ONE

Alex stomped on the ice, stuck out her tongue, and laughed at Michael.

Coward.

"Worrywart! Worrywart! Michael is worrywart! Michael is a worrywa—"

There wasn't enough time for her to hear the ice crack before the freezing river water stopped her heart.

Panic took over as her heart lurched back to life, pounding like the water on the surrounding rocks. The Darren River flowed from the mountains, and by the time the water reached the camp, its velocity loosened the jagged rocks along the shore.

Grab something. Stop yourself. This is not *happening. Not like this.*

Alex frantically grasped at the ice with her fingernails, but the river dragged her away from the open area and Michael. She flailed about before grabbing hold of a sharp piece of ice, but a second later, she was tumbling like a leaf through the rapids. Her lungs burned; there was a light coming through the ice ahead, but she couldn't hold her breath anymore.

No! Please!

Her body forced her to inhale, and as she did so, the water froze her to the core, plunging her into darkness.

The next thing she knew, sharp pain radiated through her chest, and she vomited water. When she opened her eyes, a head of blond hair and a pair of bright blue eyes stared back at her.

"That's my girl," a strange boy whispered. "You can't leave. You're going to be much too important to him."

"Who?" Alex asked in a rough whisper.

His face tunneled into blackness, and he vanished.

Michael was talking now. His voice sounded far away. His hands felt her chest, looking for injuries.

Ian, the camp's leader, cursed, and footsteps pounded toward her. A familiar scent of pine and musk teased her nostrils as Stefan scooped her up and ran back to camp.

Stefan? I'm sorry.

I'm freezing.

Her teeth chattered, and every part of her little body hurt. She rubbed her arms vigorously, burrowing beneath the blankets. The wool scratched her bare chest, and she realized she was wearing different pants. They were softer than her usual ones.

Where are my clothes?

"Ferflucs, Ian! You let my nine-year-old sister run off without telling me?" Stefan was furious, his pale skin turning redder by the second. Alex slunk further down, hoping he wouldn't notice she had awoken.

"Since when do you *not* trust Michael to watch out for Alex?" Ian snapped. "You've trusted him with her since the day she brought him home."

Alex finally opened her eyes. She hated that they were fighting because of her. Stefan's messy red hair and tear-streaked cheeks made her stomach sink. For five years now, he'd been masquerading as her brother to protect her, and she'd never seen him this upset. Ian had tied back his long black hair, and his brown eyes regarded Stefan with unfamiliar ferocity.

Stefan said, "She fell through the ice, Ian. Michael said she wasn't breathing. She was—" He swallowed hard, and his lip quivered.

I was what? Was I dead? What can't I remember?

Stefan was seven years older than Alex, but right now, he was a small, scared boy trapped in the body of a strong, brave sixteen-year-old.

Suddenly, he whipped his head toward her. "Alex? You're awake." Stefan raced to her bed and put a hand on her forehead. "How do you feel?"

"Cold." Guilt settled deep in her chest, and even under eight blankets, her body trembled as if she were standing outside in the January air.

How am I so cold?

"I told you, she needs body heat. Blankets won't cut it," Ian said.

"Fine. Can you fetch Michael?" Stefan asked. He pulled off his shirt and climbed under the blankets with Alex. The door banged shut as Ian left their hut.

"You stink," Alex said as she tried to wriggle away from Stefan, but he was too strong and she was too weak and tired.

"Sorry, Alex. You need to warm up *fast*, and the blankets aren't doing it." Stefan wrapped his arms around her and pulled her into a bear hug. His chest was like fire against her back. She soon stopped trembling, and her teeth chattered less.

Minutes later, the hut door opened again. Michael threw his shirt on the floor and snuggled against her front. Within a minute, Alex's teeth stopped chattering, and she fell asleep, snuggled between the two boys she loved like brothers.

DESPITE THE MOUNTAIN OF BLANKETS, Alex shivered in the frosty morning air. The rough wool felt like needles on her skin, but it was all they could afford. She never told Stefan how much they made her itch and chose instead to wear her thickest shirt to bed. Now, having slept without it, it was as if her skin was trying to crawl off her.

She slipped out of the blankets and gripped herself. Her hut was empty, but her clothes lay on a small dilapidated table. After pulling the thick shirt and Michael's outgrown tunic on, Alex felt more like herself. She breathed, pulling her damp braided brown hair out of her shirt.

Something feels off.

Alex threw her frayed winter cloak over her shoulders and shoved her feet into Thomas's old boots. When she stepped out of the hut, silence engulfed her. Snow had fallen while she slept, and more was coming down. Alex looked around and realized there were no footprints visible, and the camp was deserted. The sky was so thick with clouds she couldn't be sure what time of day it was.

Alex pulled her cloak close as she reached the camp's central open area. Snow crunched beneath her boots as she moved away from the row of huts behind her. Someone had sealed them up tight and locked the stable too.

We never lock the stable.

Alex's eyes widened as she looked again. A familiar older boy had appeared just ahead and was watching her. There was a connection to him she didn't have with the camp boys. There wasn't a single footprint anywhere near him. His golden hair glittered despite the lack of sunlight, and it sparked a memory from long ago.

I know that blond.

Alex took a few steps toward him, but he held up a ghostly pale hand before peering into the woods across the clearing. Closer now, Alex recognized him. He was the one who'd gotten her out of Warren after her grandfather had murdered her mother. Without him, she'd be dead.

But you're *dead.*

Prince Daniel of Datten had died five years ago. Now, seeing his face from the side, she realized she'd seen it hundreds of times out of the corner of her eye, but it had always vanished when she'd turned to look.

A low guttural growl resounded through the camp. Turning to the opening between the stables and the fire pit, Alex spotted the glowing eyes of a predator crouching, watching her. She swallowed hard.

"Alex." Stefan's voice carried across the clearing from the armory.

Afraid to move, Alex turned her head enough to spot Stefan, Ian, and Michael at different huts and buildings. They had their doors open and were beckoning her to come.

I'm too far away. I'll never make it.

Daniel moved soundlessly across the snow and positioned himself between her and the beast. The wolf's glowing blue eyes followed him.

How can it see him?

Another growl rumbled out of the wolf, making Alex step

back. Fear flooded her veins, and she bit her bottom lip so hard she tasted blood.

Daniel inched toward the wolf. In the distance, Stefan's mouth was moving, but Alex's pounding heart drowned out every sound around her. Ian leaped from his hut and began shouting, but the wolf's eyes stayed fixed on Alex.

Time slowed down for Alex when the wolf crouched again. From the corner of her eye, she could see Stefan and Ian screaming at the wolf even if she couldn't hear them. Oliver blocked Michael from running toward the standoff. Daniel remained in the beast's path, and Alex's pulse quickened as each second passed, waiting, worrying, wondering what would happen next. Then heat erupted from Alex's core as the cacophony of noise from her friends suddenly exploded. Her ragged breathing resounded in her ears, and her skin burned as she threw her arms up.

Then she heard a yelp as a massive wind tore through the camp, making Alex turn her head and protect her eyes.

When she turned back to the beast, her arms glowed. Lowering them, she curled her hands into fists, awestruck.

They're gold.

She opened her hands, wondering if this would end the glowing, but it didn't. She turned her gaze back to Daniel, who winked at her. The wolf was struggling to get up. Alex's lungs were on fire as she gasped for air.

Breathe. How am I glowing?

The wolf had righted itself and was growling again. Ian's powerful arms grabbed her biceps, and he dragged her backward through the snow toward his hut. Alex watched the wolf but Ian jumped in front of her.

"Stay behind me."

Alex peeked around Ian. The wolf was limping, its front left paw raised.

"I'm scared."

"I know. When I say 'go,' run to Stefan. Don't think. Just get over there. You hear me?"

"Yes," Alex said. Her voice trembled, her lip quivered, and her hands were still glowing gold. Ahead of her, Stefan smiled weakly at her and held out his arms, but he kept a steady eye on the wolf.

"Run!" Ian shouted so suddenly that Alex tripped, catching herself at the last second. Then she ran as hard as she could toward Stefan. As she got closer, his eyes widened in terror. Alex's breath burst from her lungs as the wolf slammed her into the ground, snarling and snapping its jaws above her. The same heat flooded her as she thrust her hands out and screamed. A yelp and several loud thumps echoed in Alex's head.

Get up. Get up!

She was glowing gold all over now. Somehow, the wind raging through the camp was coming from *her*. Wind tossed the wolf about like a leaf in a fall storm, and as the tempest roared, she soon saw Ian on the ground nearby while Stefan strained against the wind pinning him to the armory. Michael fought to get to her. Alex stumbled to her feet and stared the wolf down. Its eyes seemed almost human. Then it suddenly turned and ran back into the bush. A few moments later, a firm hand gripped her shoulder.

"Why are you glowing?" Ian asked as the wind died.

"I don't know."

"*How* are you glowing?" Oliver asked as he arrived with Michael.

"I don't know," Alex repeated.

Michael took hold of her glowing hands. His skin was hot, and as she looked up at him, her glow vanished. He smiled at her.

"Are you okay?" he asked.

Alex nodded as he hugged her.

"What was that?" Graham asked, arriving with Stefan. "How are you Stefan's sister but also a sorceress?"

I can't tell you. Stefan, what do we say?

Alex swallowed. They deserved the truth; but she didn't even understand what was going on. How could she explain it to them?

Ian patted her shoulder and looked at Stefan. "Alex came from an affair, didn't she?" Ian's tone was calm, conversational even, without a hint of question, as though he were simply commenting on the weather.

"A what?" Alex asked as everyone turned to Ian.

"You're from Datten. Your mother had an affair with that sorcerer, Merlock, didn't she?" Again, it did not sound like a question. "That's why she's dead."

Stefan's eyes darkened as he regarded her briefly before turning to Ian. He frowned and breathed deeply.

You don't have to do this!

"Yes. My father discovered Alex wasn't his and killed our mother in his rage. I took her away before he could hurt her. That's how we ended up here."

"Ian, they can't stay," Graham said. "She's dangerous."

"No, she isn't. We all have pasts we're trying to escape," Michael said.

"And she's so little," another said. The rest of the camp now surrounded them.

Ian gazed down at Alex, crossing his arms. His hard stare always made her feel extra small despite her already being the smallest in the camp.

Stand up to him. He won't throw us both out.

After a few minutes, Ian turned to the others. "She has a magical necklace that makes her look like a boy, and you're surprised to learn there's magic *inside* her too? No one knows where she is, so we will continue to keep her hidden. She's one of us for as long as she wants to be."

Alex sighed when Ian squeezed her shoulder. Stefan gripped her cheeks and kissed the top of her head. "I suspect you have questions."

"Many," Alex said.

So I am a sorceress like my mother?

"You two clucking hens can stay here, but I'm going to find that wolf," Graham said. "I don't know what you did, but I think I can track it and sell the hide."

"Take Oliver with you," Ian ordered. "No one goes out alone with that thing around."

Michael exchanged a look with Stefan.

"I've got her," Stefan said. "You help Ian check on the camp." Michael hugged Alex and hurried after Ian.

Stefan's hand slipped around Alex's shoulder and pulled her toward their hut. Once inside, he closed the door and turned to Alex.

"Could *she* do that?" Alex asked before Stefan could even open his mouth. The notion glued her to her spot right inside the doorway.

Stefan ruffled his hair and then hers before sitting on his bed. He motioned for her to sit on her bed. Instead, Alex kicked off her boots and sat beside him, curling her legs beneath her as she looked up at him. Stefan swallowed hard.

"Your mother was the Princess of Warren and had magical abilities, as you know. But I never told you *how* powerful she was. Or that sorcerer's powers don't manifest until you're older. At least, that's what I was told."

"Why didn't you tell me?"

"Honestly, no one knew if you'd get powers. There isn't a

lot of information on half sorcerers. I didn't want you to have to worry about this until you had to."

Alex looked down and picked at her shirt hem. "Is that why he killed her?"

"We don't know how many people know he did it, and I don't know why your grandfather murdered your mother. I just know I swore I'd protect you until my dying breath, and yesterday, I failed at that job," Stefan said as he rubbed his legs with his palms.

Alex grabbed his hand and squeezed it. "I'm sorry. I'll try to stay out of trouble. I know keeping us fed is hard enough."

Deep laughter filled the hut as Stefan looked at her. "You're a nine-year-old girl. You're going to get into trouble. I just need to get better at predicting *what* you'll get into."

"Are you okay with the story they came up with?"

"I'm not thrilled with the idea of my father being seen as a merciless killer, but it fits, so *we're* stuck with it."

"What if this is just the start?"

"What do you mean?" Stefan asked.

"Could I get other powers?"

"Don't worry about that. We can't change what's coming, and besides, Merlock isn't very strong. I doubt you'll get many more powers." Stefan chuckled, pulling Alex into a tight hug. "And even if you do, you'll never scare me away, you little imp."

WITH GREAT POWER COMES NAGGING BROTHERS

ALEX—SPRING 1544

Run faster!

Alex ran as hard as her legs and lungs would propel her. Branches bit her face and ripped at her clothes and satchel, but she wouldn't let the late spring foliage slow her desperate steps. Each day for the last year, Ian, Stefan, and Michael had been training her to protect herself. She could now fight a little, ride bareback, use a bow almost as well as Graham, and run like the wind. Today, she needed that speed because a life depended on it.

As she leaped over a rotten log, her magical pendant that disguised her as a boy clung to the sweat on her chest. The disguise wasn't all that impressive—all it did was make her wavy chestnut-brown hair short and rusty red. Stefan assured her that as she grew into womanhood, it would seem more impressive. That's what Daniel had told him on the day she arrived at the house of Stefan's family all those years ago. The prince had ordered them to keep her safe and never tell a soul who she was.

Alex burst out from the trees and barreled toward Kirsh. The old wooden bridge outside the town bounced as she thundered across it before reaching the worn dirt road that led into the heart of the small village. Alex ignored various onlookers as she made a beeline for the inn. Ian was in town today, learning how to manage the inn from Royce—the father of his sweetheart, Irma. She would know where Ian was.

Alex dodged the miller, who was arguing with the carpenter about when he'd be available to fix a rotten beam at the mill, but in her haste, she ran into the apothecary, nearly knocking him over.

"Look out, Alex!" he shouted.

"Sorry, Francis!"

Alex threw open the inn door and tore into the room. Weaving through the tables, she bumped into the group of mostly blond young men crowding the bar and talking to Royce.

"Watch where you're going, boy," a middle-aged man said. Alex looked up at the blond-haired man who bore the Datten knight's crest. He had green eyes, and Alex smiled. Green eyes were rare in Datten, so whenever she met someone with eyes like hers, she remembered. The boys looked at her and snickered.

What are you laughing at?

Alex spun toward them and scowled. Dressed as simple peasants, their clothes were all wrong—clean and in perfect condition. Alex's shirt was stained thanks to its previous owner, Michael, and she had patched her pants from when Thomas had fallen out of that tree. She rolled her eyes. Rich young men dressed as poor country boys.

Honor rite.

Every April, Datten would take junior knights from the castle in small groups and drop them off in various villages, and they would then work together to find their way home. If they returned within a week, the reward was priceless: an opportunity to train as a royal guard, the most prized position in all of Torian. But if they took too long or got separated, the most they could hope for was to become knights. Most were sons or nephews of royal guards and used to living in luxury. The real challenge was being stripped of money and status and having to rely on their wits to succeed. But, living in Kirsh, Alex knew the truth—over the years, it had become a complete farce. The villages all knew who they were and helped them, though tradition kept the boys in the dark.

Another stupid Datten tradition.

Alex growled at the three boys who had snickered at her clothes; the fourth one didn't even notice her. He stood next to the knight, scanning the inn with a wholly disinterested look in his eyes.

"Good luck with the honor rite," she told them. "You're going to need it if you can't even fool a poor boy from Kirsh."

Slipping under the bar, Alex rushed up to Royce. Breath finally slowing, she blurted out the entire story. "Michael fell off his stupid horse again, and it bolted. I think he broke his ankle or worse, and I can't carry him. I need Ian. Where *is* he?"

Before Royce could answer, another man replied, "The lads can help you. What good would they be as knights if they didn't help a young boy in trouble?"

"Thank you, but my brother's enough," Alex said, turning toward the older man. Her stomach lurched as her heart stopped.

The man who had spoken had black hair and a dark complexion. He stood beside the other senior knight, dressed in the same fancy kind of crested knight shirt, but he bore the crest of another kingdom—not Datten but Warren. His face was one Alex would never forget.

The king.

When he smiled at her, an ice-cold shiver crept up her spine, bringing to mind the terror of the day she fell through the ice. He looked so much like her father to begin with—same dark brown complexion, the face she missed and dreamed of so often, but the smile especially made her want to cry.

The eyes were a different story, however. Her grandfather's eyes were a dark, rich brown while her father's were blue like the sea beside their home. Before her stood the man who had taken her mother's life and forced Alex into hiding. He stared at her, oblivious to the terror raging through her, antagonizing her with her father's smile. The King of Warren had disguised himself as a knight.

She gulped.

A familiar heat soon replaced the cold flooding her veins. She tried to calm the pounding of her heart.

Breathe. He can't tell it's you.

She turned to the young men beside him.

"Thank you, but I'm fine." Her voice trembled as she spoke.

"These boys are hoping to be royal knights one day. Helping people is what we train them to do," he said.

Irma appeared in the kitchen doorway. "Then they shouldn't be laughing at a peasant boy's hand-me-down clothes."

Royce looked relieved to see his daughter. "If you get these fine men some lunch, I'll fetch Ian from the butcher, and we'll get Michael. Alex, where did he fall?"

"By the giant mossy rock. Ian knows the one."

"Perfect." Royce ruffled Alex's hair and moved around the bar. "Go into the kitchen and get yourself some lunch. You're growing like a weed."

Alex didn't need to be told twice. Once the door swung shut behind her, she let herself fall apart.

Six years I've been hiding, and he shows up the one time Stefan stays home. Breathe. No magic.

Panic soon engulfed her as her breath quickened. Then, mercifully, a pair of loving arms wrapped around her.

"Father and Ian will find Michael and bring him home. You don't have to be scared."

Alex turned and hugged Irma back, releasing all her terror about her grandfather, all her fear for Michael after he'd hurt himself. Irma rubbed Alex's back for a few moments, then turned toward the pot over the fire. The inn's kitchen was small with a work table and a smaller one beside the back door that led to the well. Alex took a stool at the larger table and watched Irma scoop stew into bowls.

"Grab me seven loaves for the basket," Irma said, pointing at the smaller table.

Alex picked them up. "Wait, seven?"

Irma winked as she grabbed six and placed them in a basket before handing the last one to Alex. Then she placed a finger to her smiling lips. Alex couldn't help but smile as she took a massive bite.

"Soudn' you geave 'em so' apples?" Alex mumbled before swallowing. Once the bread hit her stomach, she sighed. April meant the stores they had saved for winter were running out, and a full belly was a rare treat.

"What?" Irma asked, laughing.

"The tradition. You sneak them food when the old knights aren't looking."

Thinking of her grandfather made her appetite disappear, but she forced another bite anyway, not knowing when she'd get a loaf to herself again.

"Grab the bags by the door. You can sneak into the stable and hide them on their horses. It'll be obvious which ones. You can tell a palfrey and courser from a rouncey, can't you?"

Alex narrowed her eyes and tilted her head, frowning.

"Sorry." Irma laughed.

Alex looked at the pile of heavy bags and sighed.

"I almost forgot," Irma said. "Your book arrived."

"The plant book?" Alex perked up. She'd been waiting months, ever since Michael had left her copy outside the night a storm rolled through the camp in January, soaking it so much that half the pages stuck together now. She rushed toward the bags and found her book under them.

"Thank you."

Irma smiled and picked up the tray that was laden with bowls of steaming rabbit stew and bread.

Alex added the book to her satchel, hoisted the four burlap sacks over her shoulder, and slipped out the back door, hurrying to the front of the inn. She waved at the blacksmith before slipping into the stable.

Even Michael could spot these horses.

The locals' horses all had standard saddles; plus, they were dirty from the recent rains and looked gaunt. At the front, however, were six of the most beautiful horses Alex had ever seen. The leather on their saddles was so polished Alex could see her reflection. She ran her finger along the soft surface of the nearest saddle.

It must be nice to be rich.

Two black horses had fewer supplies. They lacked the rolled-up blanket the brown and gray horses had. Alex began lifting the saddlebags loaded with supplies and tying the burlap sacks under them. She found a good place on the third horse to hide the bag when someone ripped it from her.

"What did you steal?"

Alex looked back at the pale blond boy. It was the one who hadn't laughed at her clothes. His were the finest of the group, and Alex remembered how the general stuck closest to him.

Your clothes are extra fancy. Is your father an earl or royal advisor?

"I didn't take anything," she said. Alex lunged for the bag, but the boy lifted it high enough that she could not reach it. Crossing her arms, she frowned.

Being small is annoying. If we were at my camp, I'd punch you —but if you cry, my murderous grandfather will come out, and I can't risk him recognizing me.

Alex swallowed to hold back her fear.

The boy sneered, then peeked inside the bag. His eyes snapped back to her, widening as he scrunched up his nose.

"There's food in here."

Alex held up the last bag before tying it to the horse. "Of course it's food. It's the tradition. The grown-ups pay double for lunch, and we sneak food onto your horses so you don't starve. No one *actually* expects you to survive alone in the bush."

"Excuse me?"

Alex held her hand out for the last bag. He handed it over, then crossed his arms and glared.

Alex was defiant. "Excuse what? Did you fart, or are you sorry for being a spoiled knight's son who can't take care of himself?"

"No!"

She couldn't help chuckling at how red his face became. Reaching into another bag tied to the third horse, she pulled out a mushroom. "Then how do you explain these?"

"We're allowed to forage on the way here. Lucas collected those fair and square."

"They're poisonous," Alex said. The boy flinched when she held the underside up to his nose. "Gray underneath is fine; black is poisonous. These are all black. You would have puked your guts up and then shat yourself to death."

The boy's blue eyes went wide as he groaned. "You can't be older than eight. What do you know about forest plants?"

Alex finished tying up the last bag before pulling her new book out of her satchel. When she looked up, her breath caught in her throat—Daniel now stood beside the boy. He smiled from ear to ear as he pointed toward the boy and back to himself several times. Daniel never spoke, though he could communicate with her through motions. Today, she didn't need them.

The resemblance was startling. Now her grandfather helping drop off *these* boys made perfect sense. The boy was Prince Aaron—Daniel's younger brother and the sole surviving heir to the Datten throne. He was the boy she'd played with while their mothers visited each other and their fathers were off fighting against the Betruger. The boy she'd once considered her best friend—a title that had since been transferred onto Michael—before her mother's death had ripped them apart. She wished she could reveal herself right then and there; instead, she clutched her book and made an impulsive decision. Daniel vanished, still smiling at his brother.

"I have a talent for plants, so obviously you need this more than me." And with that, she handed Aaron the book.

"I can't pay you for this. Those are the rules. No gold."

"I've lived here long enough that I know the rules."

"How long?"

"I'm almost eleven. Not eight."

"Then why are you so small?"

Alex already knew she was scrawny for a girl her age, but as a boy, she must have looked downright tiny.

You won't care.

"We're poor. There isn't always enough food."

Prince Aaron had always been thoughtful, but years in the

castle would certainly have hardened him, Alex thought. But as he looked her up and down, her cheeks warmed.

"Why?" he asked. "Datten has so much farmland. There should be enough food to go around."

"You live near the castle."

"How did you—?"

"Only nobility and knights' sons take the honor rite. In the south, the crops grow better. Up here, the storms kill most of the plants. What's left is expensive, so kids are smaller."

"Why don't your parents ask for help?"

Alex looked down, kicking some hay. "My father isn't here, and my mother's dead."

Aaron's face went pale. "I'm sorry."

"It's fine. My brothers and I take care of each other, but with so many of us, if we can't forage or hunt enough food, we don't eat. Winter's rough, but come back in fall, and we'll all have put on a good amount of summer weight."

"I can't take this book." Aaron held it out to her, but Alex shook her head.

"It's fine. I have another one. It's just old. Those three you are traveling with are idiots. They'll get you killed. You must be important, so that would be bad."

"Why do you say that?"

"Because your guard is coming to check on you. When you get back to your easy castle life, remember not everyone in Datten has it as good as you."

Aaron turned to the inn, and Alex slipped out the stable's back door. As she neared the front door, she could hear Aaron talking to the knight about what he'd learned from her, asking if it was true. Alex snickered, knowing she had put questions into his head. She hurried back to the inn to get her rabbit stew.

She'd finished her second bowl when Royce and Ian arrived

with Michael and Stefan. Michael had only sprained his ankle, but he had a nasty bump on his head. Ian had rushed to camp to get the wagon, but halfway there, he found Stefan already coming with it. He'd been searching for Alex and Michael. When she saw Stefan's pale face, Alex knew they'd seen the knights leaving Kirsh. Without a word, he grabbed her arm and pulled her out of the kitchen and into the major stretch of town. It was still afternoon, and with everyone at their jobs, the streets were quiet. The skies were darkening; a storm was barreling down from the mountain, and Alex's stomach flipped at the idea of having to tell Stefan what happened that day. He nodded to the odd villager who passed by but never released her arm. Stefan led Alex to the bridge overlooking the Darren River where no one would hear them speaking. He knew she liked to watch the water even after what had happened on the ice.

After a few minutes of watching the ducks on the river-bank, he spoke. "What happened today?"

Alex swallowed hard and leaned on the railing, keeping her eyes on the ducks. Methodically, she told Stefan about her day, leaving out the part about seeing Daniel and talking to Aaron alone. When she looked up, he'd gone rigid.

"He was here? Your grandfather was in Kirsh?" Stefan asked through rasping breaths.

Alex nodded.

I don't want to talk about him.

A familiar combination of worry and determination marked his face as he grabbed her hand, pulling her from the bridge so hard she almost tripped.

"Let me go."

"We have to leave. Get you back. Hide you," he said, tightening his grip on her wrist.

"It's fine. He's not coming back."

Stefan spun around, eyes narrowed, and leaned down until their noses almost touched. "And how do you know that?"

"Because he disguised himself as a knight. He was here for the honor rite, but now they've left, and he won't be back."

"Why would the king come for the honor rite?"

Alex tugged on her shirt hem and looked down. "Because a crown prince needs a general and a king to take part?"

Stefan's face went ashen as he released her hand. "Arthur *and* Aaron were here? You saw them both?"

Alex gulped. "I talked to Aaron."

"You did *what*?"

"He didn't recognize me. I had my pendant on the entire time. I didn't realize who he was until we were alone. He followed me to the stables when Irma asked me to tie on the secret food bags."

"Alex—"

"He didn't know who I was. I gave him my plant book, and he left."

"It took us forever to save enough for that book."

"I know. But they picked the black bush mushrooms."

They'd have gotten him killed, and he's my friend. Or was.

Stefan groaned and ran his hands through his hair. "He's my father's responsibility. Not yours."

"I know, but—"

"No, Elizabeth. No buts!"

Stefan only used her royal name to make her be quiet, but today, that wouldn't work. Her temper was roaring to life, and she took a moment to steel herself for their inevitable battle.

"It was *my* book. I'm allowed to do what I want with it. You didn't want to make the trip into town with Michael and me, and now you're mad about how I handle myself when something goes wrong? I was alone because *you* weren't here.

Michael got hurt. And when I saw him—you're lucky I didn't send everyone flying across the village."

"Not so loud."

Exhausted and frightened from everything, Alex grumbled as the storm's rain fell on them, soaking her on top of everything else. Alex hadn't even gotten to talk to Michael before Stefan dragged her from the inn. Her temper was flaring as heat spread through her abdomen.

Stefan opened his mouth to speak but stopped. Alex glanced down at her glowing hands.

No. Not again.

As she glared at Stefan, lightning cracked beside them in the river. Alex cried out when a massive gust of wind blew her to the other side of the bridge. The rain came down in sheets as thunder rumbled.

Stefan rushed to her and grabbed her shoulders. "Alex, calm down."

"Stop telling me what to do!" Alex ripped herself from Stefan's grasp and shoved him as hard as she could. She caught him off balance, and he stumbled. As she thrust her arms out to keep him back, an intense heat she'd never known before flooded down her arms, making them glow brighter, and just as Stefan opened his mouth, lightning struck the river again. Alex screamed, pulling her still-glowing arms back. Across the river, the mill erupted in flames. The heat in her arms became so intense that her sleeves remained dry despite the pouring rain. Alarm bells sounded as men raced out of every building. Stumbling backward, Alex bumped into Ian and Michael. When Michael squeezed Alex's shoulder, the gold color left her arms. She watched in horror as the winds intensified, further engulfing the mill in flames.

"You have them?" Ian shouted over all the noise.

"Go help Royce," Stefan barked in reply, pulling Alex

between himself and Michael. Leaning against the bridge railing, Michael grimaced, trying to hide the pain as he grabbed Alex's hand reassuringly.

Villagers rushed around, trying to extinguish the fire. They had built the mill along the water so the river's power could run the millstone, but even with men along the river passing pails of water down multiple lines, the wood was burning too fast.

"Stefan?" Alex asked.

"No."

"But—"

"Absolutely *not*," Stefan said.

Alex put her hand on his elbow, but he quickly shoved Alex behind him.

"I can help," she whispered.

"Alex, be quiet," Michael said.

Peeking around Stefan, Alex spotted the miller, and in that moment, her heart sank. Despite his home and business burning to the ground behind him, his wide, terrified gaze remained locked on them as he stumbled backward.

"He saw," Stefan whispered.

Just then, Ian hurried over. Already drenched from helping with the fire, he pulled Alex out from behind Stefan. "Weather, premonition dreams, and now fire. How are we going to hide this one?" Ian asked.

"I don't know, but we're going back to camp *now*." Stefan's voice broke as he gave the order.

"Ferflucs. You want to ride in this storm?" Ian cursed as he scooped Alex up and started toward the stable. Michael limped after them, helped by Stefan.

"Am I in trouble?" Alex asked, terrified to hear the answer.

"No. Unless you use them on purpose, we'll never get upset

with you for your powers. They're a part of you. But we will need to keep you away from town for a while."

"What about my knitting with Irma?" Alex asked as Ian stood her beside the wagon.

"You're worried about a scarf? You set the mill on fire. I need to get you back to camp before people ask questions."

Alex swallowed the lump in her throat. "I never get to say thank you to Stefan for helping me every time I mess up. I just want to give him something for once."

Ian turned to her. "I'm sure I can convince Irma to come out to help you once things calm down here first."

Michael and Stefan arrived, and Ian helped Stefan get Michael into the wagon. Alex climbed in beside him. She couldn't stop thinking about the fire and worrying about what this new power would mean for them all if she couldn't get it under control.

I wonder if it's possible to lock away your feelings.

FINDING HIS PLACE

AARON—FALL 1546

"How late do you think they'll be?" Aaron crossed his arms and sighed as he looked out his bedroom window. Far below in the town where the higher nobility of Datten lived, the stone homes had already gone dark.

Megesti sat on the massive four-poster bed. He looked around twenty, but sorcerers aged differently. Megesti looked the same today as he did when Aaron's father was born, no wrinkle in sight on his tanned face.

His nose buried in a book, Megesti barely glanced up before replying. "We finished dinner hours ago, so I expect they'll be late. Why are you staying up? Your father will arrive tonight whether you are awake or asleep."

"The last time he arrived, I didn't even see him before he left to go back to the southern kingdoms with Jerome. Tonight, he's going to see me whether or *not* he wants to."

"Your father's busy, Aaron. The southern kingdoms are getting ever more demanding about trading alliances, and when he isn't dealing with them, the Betruger are up to something."

Aaron paced around his bedroom, deftly avoiding a pile of riding clothes and books strewn on the floor.

Mother would be appalled if she saw this mess. Good thing she doesn't come up here anymore.

In the nine years since Daniel died, Guinevere had only come up a handful of times and only when Aaron was ill and her maternal instincts overrode her grief.

"I don't care if he's busy. Jerome should be here for Jessica's birthday."

"Why do you care if General Wafner is here for his daughter's birthday? Are you sweet on her?"

Aaron scoffed.

Was that an accusing tone in his voice?

Ever since he'd turned sixteen in the spring, everyone had been asking which maiden caught his attention, but he had better things to do than chase after the silly daughters of Datten's nobility. He flicked the back of Megesti's book to close it.

"No. She's the general's only surviving child, so my father should care. But he doesn't. He probably doesn't even know it's her birthday."

The sorcerer glared and tapped the back of the book; it fell open to his page again. "Exactly. General Wafner's daughter. From a proper Datten family."

"Catch your tongue. We've been friends since the fire, and that's all we're going to be."

Megesti sighed, shook his brown hair out of his face, and closed his book. "It's for the best. It isn't as if General Wafner would approve of you."

"Jerome likes me more than my father most days. But I have other plans."

"Still holding out for my cousin, are you?"

"No," Aaron said, turning away as he blushed.

"Liar!"

As Megesti spoke, Aaron squinted into the darkening sky. When he spotted the men arriving, he spun around and clapped his hands. "Time to greet the king."

Megesti nodded and stood, handing Aaron the crown he'd left on the bed. Aaron plopped it on his head, then hurried down the west tower's spiral stairs until he reached the castle's first floor. At the bottom step, he rushed to his mother's suite. The young lady who answered the door had fiery red hair. She cocked her head and smiled.

"Jessica, dear," said a voice from inside the room, "who is it?"

Jessica turned and held the door open for Aaron. "It's His Highness."

Aaron stepped into his mother's receiving room where Guinevere sat on her gold velvet couch with her needlework. She'd swept her graying blonde hair up in a tight braid, but her blue eyes had the same youthful sparkle as Aaron's.

"Is everything all right, darling?" She placed her needlework beside her and came over to them.

"They're back. I spotted the men entering town and came to escort you two to the courtyard." Aaron bowed, making Jessica snicker and his mother smile.

"What a lovely gesture, dear. Thank you."

Jessica hurried to a small table beside the couch and returned with a beautiful crown trimmed with rubies and diamonds, which Aaron accepted and placed on his mother's head. Then he held one arm out to his mother and the other to Lady Jessica. Delighted, his mother accepted, though Jessica rolled her brown eyes before accepting.

When the three of them arrived in the courtyard, the

leaders were just entering the massive drawbridge gates, but the men were in good spirits.

"It seems the visit to the Kingdom of Hessen went well," Guinevere said.

"It does. The men aren't as tired as I thought they'd be," Aaron said.

The men dismounted and handed their reins to the squires, who were running around the courtyard. Aaron spotted his father with the last few men, though, in truth, King Emmerich was hard to miss. Aaron was already taller than his father, but while he was lean and muscular, his father was heavy and aging. Their similarities stopped at their striking blue eyes and the particular shade of golden hair passed down through the Datten royal line since the kingdom's founding. Aaron's features and pinkish skin came from his mother. He grimaced when Emmerich handed his horse to a stable boy and ruffled the lad's hair as the boy led the stallion away. His father never showed him affection or even praised him, and yet he'd give it to any squire or knight who'd had a hard day. Aaron sighed as Megesti suddenly elbowed him. "Let it go."

"Jessica?" Jerome asked. "Is everything all right?" He handed his horse to a squire and hurried over.

At the queen's side, Jessica remained composed as always. "Of course. We came to welcome you home."

Jerome bent down so she could kiss his cheek. The General of Datten towered over many people, Aaron included, but especially over Jessica, who had always been a short child.

"What a lovely surprise. Have you been behaving yourself in a manner befitting your station?"

"Of course," Jessica replied.

"Don't tease her, Jerome," Guinevere said. "Lady Jessica has better manners than any woman at court. I adore her company, and I'd choose her over my other maids any day."

"Don't let them hear you saying that," Aaron said, "or they'll take it out on her needlework—that would devastate Lady Wafner."

Jessica turned her nose up at Aaron's teasing remark. Once they were alone, she would get her revenge, but in public, she was proper.

"I wish you'd teach my son manners, Lady Jessica," Emmerich said. When he arrived, Jessica curtsied, and Megesti bowed. "I had hoped having you around more would make him behave better."

Aaron nodded. "Welcome home, Father. It seems your trip was successful."

"It was. But Hessen borders our lands—they're always the easiest to deal with. It's Bearen and Madras that put up the stink. They'll be next and will take significantly longer." Emmerich stretched, and Jerome helped him out of this armor. "They're being so ferflucsing difficult that Arthur has insisted on being present at the meetings."

"Arthur? He's been ill for years," Guinevere whispered. "Is he up for a trip like this?"

Emmerich replied in a hushed tone, "I've sent Merlock to Warren to help him travel to Bearen. It'll be easier if he can crack there. He may not like the way sorcerers travel, but it will be safer in his condition."

"Does this mean he's getting better?" Aaron asked.

"No. Worse, in fact. Arthur said he doesn't care how weak he is. He doesn't trust Edward and me to handle something this important," Emmerich said.

"When do you leave?" Guinevere asked.

"Tomorrow morning," Emmerich said.

"Many of the men have been away from their families for some time, so we'll be changing who comes with us," Jerome added.

Guinevere sighed. Jessica smiled and looked down.

"What of the king's family? Don't we deserve to see you?" Aaron asked.

His parents ignored him. Emmerich kissed Guinevere's hand, and a small smile spread across her lips.

"Flirting won't keep you out of trouble, Your Royal Highness," she said.

Aaron groaned and looked away. Everyone besides their small group had gone. Few families in Datten witnessed his mother speak to his father as an equal. Datten's king was a force of nature throughout Torian, a mountain of stubbornness as wise as the sea was old and as feared as a raging mountain storm. No one would dare to talk back to the King of Datten.

Except his mother.

Guinevere had been born Warren nobility. Her brother was an earl on the King of Warren's council. She could trace her family back to the founding families. Publicly, she was beautiful, quiet, and always at her husband's side supporting *his* decisions. But behind closed doors, her stubborn streak nearly matched Emmerich's, and she never hesitated to tell him he was wrong. Aaron enjoyed it when this happened, and his mother knew it.

Now, though, she placed a hand on the king's shoulder and smiled in a way that made Aaron's stomach churn.

Ew. Not right now.

"You've been traveling for a month with these meetings," Guinevere said.

Emmerich grinned mischievously. "You knew how busy my job was when you agreed to marry me. Jerome, will you be joining me for dinner?"

Jerome looked at Jessica and smiled. "I'd like to spend the evening with my daughter."

She tried to hide her blush as Jerome held his arm out to

his daughter. Jessica asked, "Will you be needing me anymore this evening, Your Majesty?"

"No, dear. Go with your father," Guinevere replied. Emmerich held his arm out to his queen. Jerome and Jessica headed back over the moat into town. Aaron nodded to Megesti and hurried after his parents as they headed into the castle.

The main hallway was deserted, so he could hear them talking. "Shall I have the kitchen prepare you dinner? There's boar."

Strong and stern, his father was only soft around two people: Aaron's mother and Aaron's godfather, Edward. "I'll eat tomorrow. I'd rather spend my time with my wife," Emmerich replied.

Aaron knew he was losing his opportunity to talk with his father, so he sped up, stomping on the marble floor to make sure they'd hear him.

"I'd like that," Guinevere said. "But first, you have other business."

"Other business?"

"Our son has been exceptionally patient waiting to have an audience with you."

"Aaron?" Emmerich turned to look at him. They had arrived at the end of the main hallway. The exits for the library, throne room, and dining hall were on one side and the entrances to the two royal suites on the other. Guinevere walked toward Aaron and kissed his cheek before turning back to Emmerich.

"Talk to our son, and *listen* for a change. I'll be waiting when you're finished. Good night, dear." She turned and headed into her room, leaving Aaron alone with his father.

Emmerich groaned, opened the door to his sitting room, and motioned for Aaron to enter. Aaron pushed his shoulders back as he strode into what effectively served as Emmerich's council room. A massive wooden table with benches took up half the space while the walls were lined with armor, weapons, and trophies from former kings. In the left corner was the massive fireplace that heated the king and queen's suites, and in the other corner were the stairs leading to his bedroom.

Emmerich slammed the door and crossed his arms, glaring at Aaron. "I'm tired and would like to spend tonight with your mother before I leave tomorrow. You have five minutes."

"You can't leave tomorrow."

"Thank you for your opinion. However, interkingdom trade negotiations are not your duty, so I'll be doing what's required of me as King of Datten. King Coilen is expecting me, and I will not leave him waiting."

"Delay two days. Long enough for Jerome to be here for Jessica's birthday." Aaron looked at his father, hoping for some sort of understanding.

Emmerich's eyes were cold and indifferent. "Birthdays don't matter. Do you think Edward and Arthur worry about the birthday of one of General Nial's daughters? She can celebrate with you and Guinevere."

"Randal's daughters have their mother and sisters to celebrate with. It's our fault Jessica only has Jerome. He's *your* general. Don't you even care that you're keeping him from his only remaining child on her birthday?"

Emmerich sighed, removed his sword belt, and dropped it on his table with an echoing thump. "It's *not* my job to care about the personal lives of my men. It's my job to keep the kingdom running and everyone safe. Was that everything?"

"You can't just ignore this. You want me to behave for my role, and that's what I'm doing. Make the lives of your men a larger priority."

"My men's *lives* are a priority, but their personal lives are not," Emmerich said, rubbing his forehead. "Though that is why I'm allowing them to swap out if they want."

"Except Jerome."

"He's my general. His job is to remain at my side. If your brother were alive, I could bring him along, but he's not. So Jerome is my only option. Unlike you, he knows his place."

Don't use Daniel against me. I already feel responsible for his death.

Aaron wiped his hands on his legs and crossed his arms.

"If you won't listen to me, how am I supposed to find *my* place?"

"You're insufferable. I'm tired of trying to get through to you. You ignore our rules, reject our way of life, refuse to take the basic training required of a knight, and yet you expect to have my ear the way your brother did. If you hope to become a modern king, then you need to know what makes a king modern and not just plan to act like your pacifist godfather if your time comes."

"If?" Aaron asked, dropping his arms to his side.

"Yes, *if*. The council and I have named my cousin, Wesley Rassgat, as my successor. In the event you cannot find your place in Datten, he will become king upon my death. You'll remain Prince of Datten, and the castle will remain your home, but he'll rule."

Mother didn't stop this?

"Why?" Aaron's curt tone paired well with his subsequent scowl.

"Because you're weak, and it will get you killed. If people believe I put a stronger man on the throne, they'll leave you alone. You'll be safe."

"You don't think I have it in me to be king?"

His father's blue eyes fixed on Aaron's face. Fear tumbled through Aaron's entire body as he waited for a reply.

"With Daniel, I *knew* what kind of king he would be. With you, I don't know. Maybe you have a real Prince of Datten buried in you, but after this long, I don't know how to get him out, and I'm finished trying. You want to be king? Prove your worth. Otherwise, the crown will go to Wesley. Now get out. We're finished, and we've kept your mother waiting enough."

Aaron stared at his father and felt his resolve drain away. Without a word, he turned and left, slamming the door behind him.

Megesti was waiting in the hallway. "Couldn't convince him?"

"No."

"Did you expect to?"

Aaron swallowed his frustration. "No." Then he smirked and turned toward his bedroom.

"Uh-oh. What do you have planned?"

"If you want to help, I'll come find you at five when I'm ready."

Megesti sighed and pursed his lips. "I'll be in the lab."

"Of course you will," Aaron said and headed up to his room.

THE CASTLE BELLS tolled five as Aaron slipped down the quiet third-floor hallway toward the sorcerer's lab tucked in the far corner. It had been ages since he'd visited this spot.

When Aaron opened the door, he gasped—hanging on the lab wall was the large painting that used to be in the throne room. "How long has this been here?" he asked, moving past the jars of ingredients that lined the shelves and remembering the time he'd broken one and released a snake.

"The Warren royals? Since Victoria died. My father only uncovered it about six months ago."

"Why?"

"Hope."

"He thinks Elizabeth is alive?" Aaron asked.

Surprised, he continued staring at his godfather, Prince Edward of Warren. The painting was of Edward, his dead wife Victoria, and their young daughter Elizabeth, the lost Princess of Warren. Victoria was Megesti's aunt, the younger sister of his father, Merlock. She'd died nine years earlier, just before Aaron's brother. Neither kingdom had recovered from the losses.

Megesti walked up behind Aaron. "He *knows* she's alive. The royals don't know this, but we sensed Victoria's death. My father had such a strong connection to her that when she died, he became violently ill. I thought he was dying, but he recovered in about an hour."

"And he can sense Elizabeth?"

"Over the years, he's had an unexplained pain here or there. We think it happens when Elizabeth gets hurt, but there has been nothing like that day."

Aaron moved closer to the painting. Edward's blue eyes, dark brown complexion, and black hair were such a stark contrast to the women in his life. Victoria had been beautiful with her brown wavy hair, pale skin, and emerald eyes, but Elizabeth had her mother's face as well as her father's brain. Even at four, she had watched Aaron as if she could anticipate his next move.

"Do you think she'll come home?"

"Eventually. They'll send me out to find her."

Aaron grimaced. "You? You don't even fight. And your magic is ... well, weak."

Sorry.

Megesti smiled. "You're right, but I can sense kin. Even as a child, I knew whenever Victoria was visiting before they announced her. My father thinks if I'm close enough to where Elizabeth's hiding, I'll sense her. We just have to wait for her powers to manifest."

"When will that be?"

"Around age seventeen."

"So three or four years."

"Exactly," Megesti said. "So what kind of mischief are you planning, Your Highness?"

Aaron grinned. "You're going to want your boots."

Aaron groaned as he struggled to push open the ancient royal barn doors. When the latch that secured the door open clicked, he turned and glared at Megesti. "You could have helped."

"You could have asked," Megesti replied, strolling into the barn. "So what exactly are we doing here?"

"My father plans to leave today, so we're going to cause a ruckus so he can't."

"With barn animals?"

"You're going to release the cows. The farmers will be livid that cows are wandering around their fields at harvest time. It'll take *days* to calm everyone down. Then they can leave—after Jessica's birthday."

Megesti sighed. "If you believe a few dozen cows in the royal crops will delay your father from political negotiations with the southern kingdoms, you are mistaken."

"We'll see. Can I trust you to let them out?"

"Yes," he replied, raising an eyebrow.

"Excellent. You go do that, and I'll finish up here."

Megesti took a few steps, then turned back. "What exactly are you going to do here?"

"It's better if you don't know."

"Aaron." Megesti's tone was a warning.

Aaron grinned. "It's fine. No one will get hurt. Now go."

Megesti pursed his lips and headed deeper into the barn, shaking his head and muttering. Aaron chuckled as he slipped out of the barn and headed to the chicken coops. It took less than an hour, but by the time Megesti came back, Aaron had accomplished his part.

"Now what?" Megesti asked, looking at the empty pens behind Aaron.

"We wait. I don't think it'll take long."

They headed across the moat into the keep and were only halfway across the courtyard when the screams began. Entering the castle, they paused at the edge of the royal suite hallways. Aaron grabbed his friend and pulled him into the east stairwell where they were out of sight.

Now the fun begins.

Guinevere stood in the middle of the hallway, clutching her nightdress and screaming, while Sir Reinhart tried to catch a young boar that was making a ruckus outside her suite.

"What in the Forbidden Lands is going on out here?" Emmerich bellowed, storming out of his room as a large sow ran down the hallway, nearly knocking the king over.

Aaron held back laughter as pigs and knights ran past them. His father's face was flushed with rage as he looked around and tried to console the queen.

Megesti turned to Aaron. "You released the other animals into the castle?"

"Not quite."

Footsteps thundered down the hall, and Jerome rushed around the corner with a piglet and chicken in hand. "Your

Royal Highness, the town is full of royal chickens." He held up the hen. Only castle hens bred by the royal birder had feathers of that deep a shade of red.

"Chickens in town and pigs in the castle!" Emmerich groaned.

Aaron's mother shrieked when another pig crashed into her.

"Guinevere, you grew up with animals. Why are you screaming?"

"My family raises horses, not feed animals. I hate pigs, especially when they make a mess in my suite."

"How on earth did all these animals get out?" Jerome asked.

Emmerich jerked his head toward Jerome. "Where's Aaron?"

"No," Guinevere said.

"Who else would do this? I wouldn't agree to his terms, so he retaliated."

"It sounds like our young prince is playing war with you, Your Royal Highness," Jerome said.

Is that a smirk, general?

An angry shout echoed down the hallway. "Emmerich! There are cows in my field!"

Aaron turned to Megesti, whose grin was larger than Aaron ever remembered seeing it. "Did you let a cow go into Nathaniel's crops?" Aaron asked.

"No." Megesti chuckled. "I let *all* the cows into his crops."

Aaron snorted as the king's cousin—a large, blond-haired, blue-eyed man—charged toward his father with his son, Wesley, close behind. The royal line in Datten spread far into the nobility, and his father's grandmother had been a Rassgat, tying them forever to this beast of a man and his horrible son.

"What do you mean *cows*, Nathaniel?" Emmerich asked.

"Wesley was breaking in a new stable boy when he saw Megesti letting cows go into our crops. Wherever he is, Aaron can't be far away."

Aaron groaned as he and Megesti glanced at each other. Wesley had been tattling on Aaron since he was old enough to talk. The idea of his father giving his crown to that horrible excuse for a Datten man made Aaron furious. Wesley was power hungry and dishonorable. If he ever became king, Datten might never recover from it. Aaron didn't like war or fighting—two things Datten stood for— but he wouldn't let the kingdom fall into ruin for his own personal gain.

"Jerome! Find my son and bring him to me."

Emmerich's outburst snapped Aaron out of his thoughts, and he swallowed hard. Jerome's brown eyes shifted and locked onto his for a moment before turning back to the king. "Yes, Your Royal Highness." He tossed Nathaniel the chicken and handed the piglet to a knight before heading into the west tower. Aaron and Megesti rushed up the east tower stairs.

When they reached the third floor, Jerome stood in the hallway with his arms crossed, but his face was soft.

"You did this?"

Aaron put his hand on Megesti's arm and nodded.

"Why would you act so foolishly, knowing how much rides on these negotiations?"

"It's Jessica's birthday tomorrow." Aaron stood tall and sighed. "I tried talking to him, but he didn't care, so I took the choice from him. He can't leave with the Rassgats screaming about lost crops and the castle full of pigs."

Jerome pursed his lips. "I appreciate you looking out for her and wanting me to be here for her birthday, but she understands my responsibilities."

"While that's true, she also would never ask you to stay,

even if she doesn't want to spend another birthday without you. I'll risk my father's wrath to give her one with you."

"Well, thank you, Your Highness," Jerome said, exhaling heavily. "But I hope you're prepared for the consequences because it won't be just your father's wrath. Warren is expecting him today. When he doesn't arrive, Arthur will come here, so it's Arthur's temper you should worry about."

"I'm not scared of Arthur," Aaron said. He crossed his arms and turned to Megesti, looking for support. Instead, he saw the blood drain from his friend's face.

"I am," Megesti said.

"What? Why?"

"Because we believe he killed Victoria," Jerome said in a hushed tone.

Aaron's stomach felt as if it were full of rocks. Hurting a member of the royal family was despicable. Aaron already knew Arthur to be heartless, but that he would go do far was still a shock even if Aaron knew how treated his own son.

If anyone is capable of such dishonor, it's Arthur.

Then he scrunched his face after a moment, lost in thought. "Who is 'we'?"

"Edward, our fathers, Matthias Veremund, both Warren generals, and Jerome," Megesti said.

"If he's responsible, why hasn't anyone done anything?" Aaron asked.

"No conclusive proof." Megesti shrugged.

"*Your* father might condemn a man with so little evidence, but Edward won't," Jerome said. "He's suspected his father for some time now. Matthias Veremund, your uncle Bernhard Strobel, and your father's cousin Kruft Rassgat started looking into things with General Bishop following her death. After someone murdered Matthias's family, Edward forbade anyone from investigating further, but General Bishop has secretly continued doing so."

"Why don't they just use the pearl?" Aaron asked.

"Arthur's will is too strong. He can show what he wants. We'd get nothing out of him," Megesti said.

"Is that why no one ever looks for the princess?" Aaron asked.

"Someone still looks for her," Megesti said.

"The day Victoria died, Arthur convinced General Bishop to send Edward and Victoria's guard, General Nial, with Edward rather than keeping him with Victoria and Elizabeth. General Bishop never got over that mistake," Jerome explained. "That night, he stepped down, and General Nial became Warren's general. Matthew Bishop has been looking for the princess ever since. He believes she's in Datten in some isolated small town whose residents would never recognize Victoria's daughter."

Aaron exhaled. A royal assassinating a family member wasn't new—Datten's past was full of men killing their own brothers to take the throne or a title—but never a daughter. Women didn't inherit titles, so murdering a princess was unthinkable. Datten stood for honor, and there was no honor in a king killing his own daughter-in-law.

"This is madness," Aaron said.

"It is. But it's also why your father won't anger Arthur. No one's sure what he is capable of," Jerome said. "Now get yourselves down to the stable."

"Stable?" Megesti asked.

"You're going to spend the day hiding. I want your father to calm down before he decides your punishment."

Aaron nodded to Jerome, then raced Megesti to the stable.

They spent the morning riding, and that afternoon, they hid in a small bar in town called the Lion's Chest. Jerome found them there at dinnertime and subsequently brought them back to the castle where Emmerich was waiting.

Megesti was first. Jerome left Aaron outside the throne room and headed inside with the sorcerer. As the doors closed, Aaron debated barging in but thought better of it. Maybe it was better to give them a few minutes. Perhaps his father would calm somewhat. After some time had passed, he took a deep breath and knocked on the door.

"Enter!" his father ordered.

Aaron pushed open the ancient doors and walked down the long path to his father's throne. The marble floor, while worn from years of use, glistened. Guinevere sat on the edge of her throne on the left side of the massive obsidian stone dais. Her blonde hair sparkled in the candlelight. His father was speaking to Jerome and Nathaniel while Wesley and Sir Kruft Rassgat stood off to the side. Megesti was nowhere to be seen. Aaron swallowed hard and raised his chin as he strutted toward his father. Even from across the room, he could already see his father's disappointment, and for one moment, he regretted his behavior.

Then Emmerich turned to him. "We have a witness placing Megesti at the scene of the crime. He claims he was acting alone. What do you have to say to his confession?"

"It was my idea. He was acting under my instruction."

"As I said," Wesley said, smirking.

Aaron glared at him while Emmerich muttered something to Nathaniel. Then his mother spoke. "What were you thinking, Aaron?"

Aaron stood tall and faced his mother. She would understand as soon as he explained, but he hated causing her pain. "I wanted Jessica to have Jerome present for her birthday tomorrow. I asked my father to delay leaving, but he refused. So I took matters into my own hands."

Surprise replaced the disappointment on his mother's face, her eyes sparkling as she pursed her lips and shook her head. Aaron recognized that look—she was proud of him but couldn't go against his father in front of the Rassgats.

Then Emmerich moved a few steps toward Aaron. He well knew the tone he was about to hear was that of the King of Datten and not of his father. Daniel had taught him the difference at a young age—pride came from their father, disappointment from the king.

"If you expect people to listen to you, then prove you are worth listening to. You earn respect through achievements and actions; it's not granted."

"But—"

"Do *not* interrupt me." Emmerich's voice echoed through the room as Aaron gulped. His mother was standing now. She exchanged a look with Jerome that sent him moving toward the king.

"You're the Crown Prince of Datten. You should be the heir to my throne, but your immature, pacifist behavior has made it impossible to give you any responsibility or proper duties as a prince. You're sixteen, for goodness' sake. By sixteen, I had been king for three years. At fifteen, your brother was well on his way to being a second to the general, and you can't even lead a group of young knights in mock battle."

"Emmerich—" Guinevere's voice cracked behind him.

"You're a disappointment."

His father's words stung. He'd always suspected his father felt this way, but now it was confirmed.

Does he wish Daniel were here instead of me? That his weak, pacifist son had died in the flames that morning?

Aaron opened his mouth to reply when the massive doors flew open so hard they struck the throne room walls. Everyone inside turned to the back of the room.

"Emmerich, why are you not on your way to the southern kingdoms? Our entire trade negotiation relies on you being punctual," King Arthur barked as he stormed up the aisle. Prince Edward followed behind in silence. Aaron glanced down when Edward's deep blue eyes met his own.

"We'll leave tomorrow, Arthur. I just need to handle a situation here first," Emmerich said.

"By 'situation,' you mean your failure to discipline that brat of a boy you call a crown prince."

King Arthur stopped walking and glared at Aaron, who stepped back. Arthur was intimidating during the best of times; when he was angry, he was the most terrifying man in Torian. Gray and white speckled his obsidian black hair, but his dark brown eyes bore into Aaron's soul. It was unreal how similar he looked to Edward but how different they were.

You murdered your daughter-in-law. You're a monster.

Arthur sneered before turning back to Emmerich. "It's that woman's fault he's so weak. If you disciplined him how I told you to, you wouldn't have these problems."

"I will not beat my son into compliance," Emmerich snapped. Aaron noticed the change in his father's stance. Before, he'd appeared relaxed, even while angry with Aaron; now, he looked like a wolf ready to pounce.

"It worked on Edward," Arthur said with a shrug as Edward walked up beside him.

"I am well aware of what your parenting did to Edward," Emmerich said, closing the distance to Arthur.

"Then stop letting him flee to Warren every time you have a fight. You're letting my son and that idiot sorcerer teach him to be a coward. Between them and your useless wife, he's never going to amount to a ferflucsing thing."

"Stop insulting my mother!"

Aaron didn't realize he was the one who had shouted until

everyone was looking at him. Arthur's stare as he stalked forward made Aaron swallow and step back.

Maybe I am scared of you.

But before Arthur reached him, Edward stepped between them.

"Move." Arthur's eyes flashed. "I intend to teach this disrespectful boy a lesson his father should have taught him years ago."

"No," Edward snarled.

"I gave you an order, Edward." Arthur stepped forward until his and Edward's noses practically touched. Edward's hands clenched so tightly that they shook. Aaron spotted his father holding back his mother. He'd never seen such rage on her face.

"And I'm ignoring it. You will not touch my godson."

Arthur growled, then stormed toward Emmerich.

"If you don't smarten that boy up soon, the day you die and he takes the crown, the Betruger will come down here and slaughter every man, woman, and child in Datten. If you don't think they've heard about how different Aaron is from Daniel, then you're a fool."

"Thank you for your input, but I have my kingdom well in hand," Emmerich said.

Arthur laughed. "You have about as much control over your kingdom as you do that boy. Now, get your men. King Coilen is not a patient man, and if you aren't coming with me, I'll negotiate without you. Don't think your army scares me. I know you won't attack the kingdom of your beloved wife and best friend. My son's friendship with you keeps you in line."

"He hasn't finished here," Guinevere said. Aaron watched his father pull her behind him.

"Catch your tongue, woman," Arthur said. "I don't listen to

your brother. What on earth makes you think I care what you have to say?"

Aaron's nostrils flared as he took a step forward, but Edward slid a restraining arm across his chest. "Your father's protecting your mother. Don't make this worse."

"Your Royal Highness?" Everyone turned to Sir Kruft Rassgat. "I volunteer to escort you to Bearen with King Arthur and Prince Edward. General Wafner could stay here and deal with the consequences of the prince's prank."

Emmerich nodded to his cousin. "Thank you, Kruft. Does that work for you, Arthur?"

"As long as we leave now, I don't care who watches your back. Now, where has that idiot sorcerer of yours gone?"

"Aaron, you're dismissed. Jerome will find you later to give you your punishment," Emmerich said.

For once, Aaron didn't argue. He turned and fled the room, trying to hide the terror he was sure was all over his face.

When he reached the safety of the hallways near his room, Aaron leaned against the wall and took a few deep, calming breaths, but he froze when Lady Jessica rounded the corner. She came to a stop in front of him, crossing her arms like her father.

"This chaos was all your doing, wasn't it?" Her brown eyes tried to pry the answer out of him.

"Yes," Aaron said. He stood taller and smiled. "Enjoy your birthday with your father."

Then he stepped around her to head to his room, where he planned to hide until Arthur left.

"Aaron."

Jessica's use of just his first name made him stop and spin around to smile at the young Lady Wafner. Always the proper lady, she only called him by his first name when they were alone, and she wanted him to pay attention to what she had to say.

"Yes, *Jessica*?"

"Thank you."

AARON OBEYED the command to stay confined to his room until the morning after Jessica's birthday. His books were enough to occupy him during that time, and knowing Jessica would spend the day with her father made the punishment worth it. But he couldn't stop thinking about what he'd learned concerning Arthur's possible or even likely involvement in Victoria's death and Elizabeth's disappearance. *How anyone could do that to their own son is inconceivable.*

After everyone had gone to bed, Aaron grabbed a small torch from the stairwell, crept into his brother's room, and searched through Daniel's books. He remembered his brother had always taken meticulous notes during his training. Eventually, Aaron found the small journal he was seeking and took it to his room.

It's a ridiculous amount of work to learn to be a knight. How did you accomplish this so young?

Like Daniel, Aaron had completed the honor rite. Three years earlier, he'd been dropped off in a penniless village by the mountains and had been required to find his way back with Caleb, Lucas, and Hunter. From Daniel's notes, Aaron knew he could check off riding and getting to know the other knights. He was already decent at running, but he'd never fought. Aaron groaned when he discovered it had taken working daily for hours with Jerome for Daniel to develop his skills with the sword. Aaron sighed, knowing he would have to work twice as hard since he was so far behind. His mind still racing, he blew out the torch, tucked the journal under his pillow, and fell asleep.

Aaron woke early. Stars were still in the sky as he crossed the courtyard toward the group of young knights. They all wanted to work inside the castle. Their fathers, grandfathers, and even great-grandfathers were castle guards, but in Datten, lineage only got you into the training sooner. Every knight who wanted to work in the castle had to prove himself in the areas of loyalty, skill, and dedication.

Lucas and Caleb flanked Aaron.

"You're late," Caleb said.

"By about three years." Lucas chuckled.

"What's so funny?"

The lads jumped and turned to face Jerome. The general's eyes grew wide when he noticed Aaron's training attire.

"Ten miles. The last man to arrive does another mile around the castle. Go!" Jerome shouted.

The boys dashed toward the keep and the massive drawbridge. Aaron turned to go, but Jerome's vise grip on his forearm held him in place.

"Is this another prank, Aaron?"

"No." Aaron pulled out Daniel's journal and handed it to Jerome. "You taught Daniel, and now I'm asking you to teach me. I don't want Datten to go to Wesley. I want the crown to stay in our line and, when the time comes, to take Arthur out. If he was responsible, I want to help make him pay for what he did to Victoria and Elizabeth and what he continues to do to Edward."

Jerome flipped through the journal and sighed. "You'll have to spend your mornings training with the castle hopefuls and then afternoons working with me one-on-one until you're ready to train with the senior knights. Then you'll work with them."

Aaron nodded.

"It won't be easy," Jerome said.

"I know. I need to make up for lost time. Don't treat me any differently than you would have my brother. Train me the same," Aaron said.

"You're a different person. I'll push you to the same precipice as I pushed him, but you need different lessons. Regardless of what your father wants, you're a different prince, and that isn't bad. Now go, or you'll be running that extra mile."

"Yes, sir." Aaron nodded and hurried to catch up with the group.

COMPROMISES AND VICTORIES

ALEX—SPRING 1547

Stefan always ruined everything. Alex exhaled, trying to control the anger coursing through her as she adjusted her footing on the branch below and hoisted herself onto another tree limb. She could still hear him screaming at her and Thomas, threatening to bury him alive in the woods if he even looked at her again. Alex understood Stefan's job was to protect her, but some days, she simply wanted to be a normal girl, to experience things thirteen-year-old girls in town could. But it was stupid.

I'll never be normal.

The warm air around her suddenly turned cold. She looked up and saw Daniel sitting on a limb, watching her. Usually Alex didn't mind when he appeared; apart from the frigid air, he didn't interfere with her life. He couldn't talk, and if she ignored him long enough, he'd go away. But today, she had had enough of older brothers controlling her life.

"Go away. I'm not in the mood to talk," she said as her leg suddenly froze. Alex glared at him, but he left his hand on her calf.

Daniel frowned, but his eyes were soft. Even without words, she knew he wanted her to know she wasn't alone. He had a knack for showing up when she felt lost and alone.

"Why are big brothers so stupid?" Alex asked. Daniel raised his left eyebrow. "Don't give me that look. You know what I'm talking about."

Daniel winked and patted Alex's leg. He tilted his head down, motioning to the ground, and waved goodbye before he vanished.

Alex sighed, closed her eyes, and leaned back against the tree trunk, unbothered when the rough bark scratched her head. Far below, a twig snapped, and the ground crunched. Alex didn't open her eyes.

Michael.

Anytime she became emotional enough to run and hide, only Michael was brave enough to follow her.

An acorn bounced off her arm.

"Did Stefan send you?" she asked. Alex considered growing some acorns to throw back, but her plant magic only worked when she was happy.

"I heard him threatening Thomas when I returned from hunting with Graham. I figured you'd be here since your horse was in the stable."

"You mean Graham's horse. I still have to share. Wait—does that mean Graham heard Stefan too?" Alex groaned, clenching her jaw and dropping her face into her hands.

"When I left, Oliver was still trying to calm Stefan down."

"Oliver knows about it too?"

"The entire camp knows, Alex. I'm sorry. Please come down. I'm here to listen to your side as your friend."

Groaning, Alex shimmied away from the trunk and lowered herself onto her stomach. A few quick leaps, drops, and swings brought Alex to the ground next to Michael.

"What does everyone know?" Alex asked.

Michael responded by wrapping her up in a hug. Annoyed, Alex tried to pull away, but Michael held her tighter.

"They know Thomas kissed you in the stable, and you didn't stop him. Stefan walked in, lost his mind, and dragged Thomas off while you chased after him, telling him to stop. When he didn't, you ran."

Alex's cheek and forehead burned as her face rested on Michael's shoulder. "Is Thomas okay?"

"Yes. Oliver calmed Stefan down before he could hurt him."

"Why is he so mad? I'm almost fourteen, and Thomas is nice. You don't have to worry about him. Stefan didn't worry about you coming after me."

Michael laughed so hard the sound reverberated throughout Alex's chest. He then loosened his grip, moved his hands to her face, and kissed her forehead.

"*That* is the closest to kissing you I'll *ever* get. I may not be blood like Stefan, but I'm just as much your brother. If anyone touches you, they have to deal with him *and* me."

Alex pulled away. Wiping her hands on her pants, she kicked a pine cone across the ground, searching for the words. As if expecting this, Michael narrowed his blue eyes, leaned against the tree, and cleared his throat.

"I'm not a little girl anymore," Alex said finally. "I should have the freedom to have some normal experiences."

"You're right. You *aren't* a little girl anymore, and that's the problem."

Alex scowled and pointed at Michael. "I swear, if you tell me what a lovely young lady I'm becoming, I'm going to hit you."

Michael chuckled. "I'm not old like Stefan. To a twenty-year-old, you're a child, but I'm fifteen, and you aren't *becoming* a woman, Alex—you *are* one. You can't pass as a boy anymore.

You've got breasts, for goodness' sake! And you're pretty—prettier than every girl in Kirsh, and the boys at camp notice. They can't help it."

"They see me as a little sister, nothing more."

"Maybe that was true when you were little, but you aren't anymore. Though if you let me cut your hair, I'm sure they'd stare at you less."

Alex glared at Michael.

"You're right," Michael said. "Thomas is a nice boy, but he's not for you."

"How do you know?"

"Would you marry Thomas?"

"No. I'm fourteen."

"Girls in Kirsh get married as young as sixteen. Village boys look for a wife when they hit eighteen, so any boy who wants to kiss you has other ideas on his mind. Meaning, if you aren't interested in marriage, then you shouldn't lead Thomas on."

"Michael—" she began, her tone a warning.

"I know, I know," Michael interrupted, throwing his hands up. "Stefan plans to find you a more fitting match, like a lord or duke. I think you could marry an earl or a prince if Stefan could get you in front of one."

I never thought of that.

Alex looked down and tugged the hem of her shirt.

Michael grabbed her pale hand in his light copper ones. "It isn't just that. We wouldn't need to worry about Thomas, which is why Stefan's making an example of him. If a nice boy is forward with you, other not so nice boys will get ideas."

"I can take care of myself."

"I know you can, but we won't risk it, won't risk you. By putting Thomas in his place, it's clear: you're *off-limits*."

"Boys are idiots," Alex said.

"Brothers are the worst." Michael's smirk enraged Alex,

and she moved to shove him, but he dodged. "Looks like you need to practice your moves."

Alex shrieked in annoyance and lunged again, but he locked his arms around her from behind. Alex squirmed and wiggled but had no luck.

"You're touching my breast," Alex said suddenly.

Michael gasped and jumped back. "I'm sorry. I didn't mean—"

Before he could finish, Alex spun around and slammed into him with her shoulder, sending him crumpling to the ground.

Michael groaned. "I didn't touch you, did I." It wasn't a question.

Alex smirked and kicked dirt on Michael's stomach. She laughed at this, but then the air left her lungs as she slammed into the ground.

"You know better than to stand so close to your victim." Michael was chuckling as he rose and held his hand out to her. Groaning, Alex sat up and took it before Michael pulled her to her feet with one strong yank.

"How do I face everyone after this?" Alex brushed the dirt off the back of her pants.

"You breathe, you put one foot in front of the other. I know you're embarrassed right now, but Stefan's behavior isn't your fault, so don't let it make you feel uncomfortable."

"And Thomas?"

"I'm sorry, but he'll stay as far away from you as possible. He's terrified of Stefan, and there isn't much we can do to change that." Michael held his palms up and shrugged.

Alex crossed her arms and glared at Michael before tilting her head back in frustration as a hot wind blew past them.

"Alex—"

"I came here to calm down. You're the one getting me mad

again." Her tone was snarkier than she'd intended; she was losing control over her anger.

"I'm sorry. I know it's easier if you get it all out. Go scream. I brought a bucket." Michael pointed to the large bucket a few feet away that Alex hadn't even noticed. "Scream all your anger out, and if something catches on fire, I'll handle it."

Oh, Michael.

Alex clenched her fists as her anger churned in her stomach like the Oreean Sea would when it came into the Darren River. For a time, she tried to slow her breathing but was unsuccessful. Alex nodded to Michael and trudged toward the Darren River. Michael's idea was practical, but he didn't comprehend the level of anger pumping through her blood.

It's not just the kiss or the yelling. It goes so much deeper than you'll ever know. I wish I could tell you everything.

Reaching the riverbank, Alex glanced back to see the panic hit Michael's face before she leaped into the freezing river. This far into the woods, the water was deep, but she knew how to avoid the strongest part of the current. When she closed her eyes, the darkness and freezing water embraced her before she opened her mouth to scream.

Hot bubbles tickled her face as she expelled every bit of air from her lungs. Then she pushed off the squishy river bed, broke the surface, and filled her burning lungs as quickly as she could.

"Alex! Out of that water, right now!" Michael shouted from the shore.

Instead, Alex took another big breath and dove back in. Three more times, she filled her lungs and screamed them empty until she could taste blood in the back of her throat. Breaking the surface one last time, Alex finally found her control. She ignored her screaming chest and lungs as she approached the riverbank where Michael was sitting. He narrowed his eyes, but Alex knew he wouldn't say anything. It was the careful balance they'd crafted over the years. Stefan was the enforcer and disciplinarian while Michael was the confidant who balanced her temper. Alex grabbed hold of the large root that hung down from the bank and pulled herself up.

Michael moaned. "How am I supposed to explain you being soaking wet?"

"Tell them I tried to drown myself in grief," she said, giggling as she threw an arm over her forehead.

Michael laughed. "Who'd believe that?"

"Fine. Tell them you did it to calm my fiery temper. Everyone will believe that."

Michael picked up his bucket and draped his arm around Alex's shoulder as they returned to camp. Alex hummed a little tune, and soon Michael joined in. As youngsters, they'd discovered only they knew these songs, creating a connection between them. They hummed and laughed the entire way, coming up with ever crazier suggestions to explain Alex being soaked.

When they arrived, every lad was staring at them. Alex sighed. "So everyone knows."

"Looks like it," Michael said, scowling. "Find Stefan. Get this over with. Otherwise, it's going to eat at you."

Before Alex could reply, the food larder door opened, and Stefan came out with Thomas. Stefan was holding the slip of parchment they used for shopping anytime they went to town, but Thomas looked whiter than the mushrooms that grew in the woods.

"Poor guy," Michael chuckled. "He still has to help Stefan with the food list, even after this morning's excitement."

Alex elbowed Michael, but when she turned back to the

food storage cellar, Thomas had vanished, and Stefan was heading for them. Alex swallowed hard.

"Go," Alex said.

"You sure? I can stay for support."

"This is between Stefan and me."

Michael patted Alex's shoulder before heading off. Alex stared at Stefan, trying to stand tall as he drew near, tilting her head up to look at him.

"So," Stefan said.

"So."

"Are you calm enough to talk about this?"

"Are you?" Alex snapped back.

Stefan raised an eyebrow.

I don't care.

Stefan studied her wet clothes, glanced around, then leaned in close. "To your room, Your Highness," Stefan said in a whisper so quiet Alex barely heard him.

Alex whipped her head around fast enough to hit Stefan's face with her sopping braid, and he sighed as she strode toward their hut. The door struck the wall as Alex stormed inside. Before Stefan even made it into the hut, she'd tossed aside her shoes and socks and replaced her wet pants. She waited until his boots hit the floor before she removed her wet shirt and threw it at him.

"Warn me next time," Stefan said, slamming the door behind him.

Footsteps sounded behind her, followed by water hitting the floor. Stefan was still wringing out her clothes as Alex sat on her bed, slipping on her dry shirt. After hanging the wet clothes on the end of his bed, Stefan sat across from her.

"What were you thinking?"

"About what, exactly?"

"Alex—"

"What happened to 'Your Highness'?" Reaching under her bed, Alex pulled out her boots and fresh socks, putting them on.

Stefan groaned and dropped his head into his hands. "How could you let Thomas kiss you?"

"So you aren't mad about me screaming in the river?"

His head snapped up. "You did *what*?"

"Michael brought a bucket with him to talk to me in case I set something on fire, but I was too angry. I would have set the entire forest ablaze. So I jumped into the river and screamed underwater to make sure my fire couldn't cause problems," Alex said, sighing as she crossed her legs.

"What is it with you and water?"

"I'm from Warren. The sea is in our blood."

"You can't just go around kissing people," Stefan said, abruptly switching gears.

"I didn't *kiss people*, Stefan. I *let* Thomas kiss me. He's nice, and I just wanted one normal thing in my life. Is that so wrong?"

Please, can you at least understand that?

"Yes, it is wrong." Stefan's brown eyes burned into her soul. "You're not some maiden from a small village. *You* are the Crown Princess of Warren. You cannot kiss people. If your father knew about this, he'd be livid."

"You don't know how my father would react. Warren's progressive, and I'll be fourteen next month. If I were home, I'd have had my first kiss ages ago."

Stefan tilted his head. "And just who do you think would kiss you, princess?"

"A prince, or at least an earl. My father betrothed me to Daniel before I vanished. I assume he would have found another," Alex whispered.

"You could marry Prince Harold of the Betruger. Put a stop to that never-ending war."

"I thought the kingdoms wanted Datten and Warren to be united?"

"If you're forced into marriage for political reasons, it might as well benefit *all* of Torian," Stefan said.

"Regardless of who I end up with, if I were at the castle, I promise you I would have kissed someone by now." Alex crossed her arms and glared at Stefan.

"Not on my watch you wouldn't have."

Alex bit her cheek to keep herself from giggling. As funny as it was to think of him trying to stop her, she knew it wouldn't help to laugh at him. "I'm sorry you feel you failed because Thomas kissed me. But I don't think you did. I'm safe, alive, and loved. Michael explained why you can't allow anyone here to kiss me, and as frustrating as it is, it won't happen again."

"I made sure it won't. Alex, guarding you is more than a duty to me now. I love you as a sister and need you safe, but I also want what's best for you. I take my job seriously, and I'll protect you as long as you'll let me."

Alex sighed. "I know, but I feel smothered. I understand you need to protect me, but it's taking too long."

I want to go home.

Stefan reached across the space between their beds. Today, that space felt enormous. Warmth flowed up her arm as he squeezed her hand.

"What do you mean, '*taking too long*'?" he asked.

"It's been nine years. Did you think we'd still be here after all this time?"

Stefan's lips pursed as he shook his head. "No. I never imagined your grandfather would make it this long."

Alex spun her hand around and held Stefan's. "What if I turn twenty and he's still alive? We can't stay here forever. You joked about protecting me from a betrothed, but at some point, I'll have to marry. How old will Warren let my father become without an heir?"

"I don't know," Stefan admitted, dropping her hand. He stood and crossed their small hut to look out the window. "Daniel told me to stay away until Arthur was dead. Until it's safe."

"So I'm just supposed to grow old alone?" Alex swallowed and looked down. Breathing out, the terror of being alone built up inside her; the soft patter of rain hitting the roof hut's roof filled the room. Alex looked up at the ceiling before turning to Stefan. He was staring at her, but his eyes were soft now.

"I know you miss him, and I know Michael and I can't replace your father, no matter how much you love us."

"Can we pick an end?" Alex looked down at her lap, rubbing her clammy palms on her pants.

The floor creaked as Stefan came over and squatted before her. "What do you mean?"

"Pick an age? When I hit it, we leave, no matter what?" Alex tried to speak with confidence, but her sagging shoulders betrayed her.

Stefan took her hands. "Where would you go?"

As Alex looked at him, a glint of gold at the front door drew her attention. Daniel winked and pointed to his shirt. The golden lions glistened even in the dim light of their hut.

"Datten?" Alex whispered.

"Deal."

Alex's attention snapped back to Stefan. "Deal?"

"If you turn twenty and Arthur's still alive, we'll go to Datten. If anyone in Torian can protect you, it would be my father and King Emmerich, especially if your grandfather doesn't know you're alive."

"Why twenty? Why not eighteen?"

Stefan sighed. "Torian expects princesses to marry at twenty-one. If Datten and Warren followed tradition, your betrothal to Daniel would have moved to Aaron. We'd come back, and you'd marry Aaron, making your safety Datten's responsibility."

So they would only protect me if I married Aaron? Where's the honor in that?

"You're the goddaughter of Datten royalty, and that might be enough. Remember, it was different last time. Daniel brought you to my family's house the day after your mother died and when no one suspected the murder involved your grandfather. You didn't tell me until years later, and we can't be certain they found out, but knowing that Arthur killed your mother? My father and I would never leave your side ..."

Alex pulled her hands back. "So six more years?"

Stefan nodded before rising. "Think you can behave for that long?"

"You know I can't stay out of trouble for six hours, let alone six years. But I promise I won't kiss any more lads."

"So I just have to make sure they don't kiss you?" Stefan asked. Alex nodded, and Stefan sighed. "I'm sorry about how I reacted this morning. How can I make it up to you?"

"I want a horse. I'm tired of sharing with Graham."

Stefan laughed. "We can't afford another horse."

"I know, but you asked."

"Oh, so you're aware how impossible this request is."

"I am, but your father would get me a horse if I asked."

"I'm certain even the Prince of Datten could manage a horse for you or at least a pony," Stefan said, playfully pushing her.

"So who do you think I should end up with?" Alex asked.

"I don't care if it's a prince, a knight, or a nobleman as long as he can protect you and handle everything you throw at him."

"I don't think there exists a prince with a forceful enough personality to take me on."

Stefan considered her for a moment. "You've inherited your mother's looks, all the logic of Warren, and your grandfather's temperament and presence."

Neither of them spoke for a while. They never said it, but Prince Edward was kind, like Alex's mother. Ironically, her temper and determination came from the man who'd taken everything from her.

"If you're finished, we can go now," Stefan said. Alex's pendant glittered in his palm.

"Go where?" Alex asked.

"To town for supplies," Stefan replied, motioning to the door.

"But I'm not on the supply run today."

"If you think I'm leaving you here with Thomas after this morning, you've lost your mind."

Alex laughed before suddenly wrapping her arms around his waist and hugging him. Startled, he hugged her back.

She sighed softly. "Thank you."

Then she snatched her pendant and slipped it over her head, and they left the hut.

ALEX ALWAYS FELT like she could fly when she rode the horses. She'd had a connection with horses for as long as she could remember. Even in Warren, she remembered how much she loved being in the stable.

Today, Alex was riding Stefan's horse while he followed in the wagon with the other horse. They arrived in Kirsh faster than usual, and when Stefan tried to get Alex to take half the list of supplies, she refused.

"You can't avoid the mill forever, Alex."

"Of course I can. *Michael* never makes me go."

"I'm not Michael," Stefan said, leaning toward her.

Alex narrowed her eyes and huffed. The day of the accident, the miller had seen her hands glowing, but lucky for her, he'd been drinking in the inn most of the day, and so no one believed him when he blamed "that fire-wielding brat" for destroying his mill. He watched her like a hawk every time she came to town, and one time, he had even yelled at her. Stefan didn't know about that.

Stefan sighed. "Cut that out. I'm not cruel. Today was traumatic enough. Ask the blacksmith about new horseshoes for Elm, and then you can go to the inn to help Irma."

Alex sighed and smiled, and after a quick glance toward the mill, she turned and ran toward the inn stables, kicking up dust in her wake. Odo the blacksmith was expecting her and went with Elm to size the horse up for new shoes. Normally, Alex enjoyed watching the men in town work with the horses, but today, she was restless. She headed into the inn's stable.

Ian was scooping out the stalls. "What are you doing in town? It isn't your week."

Alex sighed, shrugged, and picked up the other pitchfork to help. Last winter, after years of apprenticing under Royce, Ian had married his daughter, Irma. Now, he lived in town, and Alex missed having him as a buffer between her and Stefan. Michael tried, but since he was afraid of Stefan, he wasn't much help.

"Boys are idiots."

Ian chuckled. "Which boy?"

"You expect me to pick just one?"

"Okay. Then just the one causing the blushing."

"I'm not—" Alex stopped working.

"Who kissed you?"

Alex whipped around. "How did you know?"

"I've gotten questions. I figured at least one had to be asking about you. And you seem dazed right now."

"I am not."

"You are. Equal parts guilty and happy, I'd wager. It was Thomas, wasn't it?"

Alex turned away, convinced her burning cheeks would set the stable ablaze.

"How badly did Stefan take it?" Ian asked.

"As bad as when my fire came in."

Ian sucked his breath in. "So you're hiding out in the stable while he gets the supplies?"

Alex turned back to Ian. "No. I'm plotting how to steal a horse since he won't get me one."

"Aren't you a little young for a life of crime?" Ian held his arms out, and Alex went for a hug. "I'll make you a deal. Clean the stable while you wait for Stefan, and I'll pay you. That can start your horse fund."

"Deal."

Alex spent hours cleaning out the stable. Once she finished, Alex watched a well-dressed man arrive at the inn. Despite what she expected, his clothes were clean and his full head of graying brown hair was neat after what must have been days of riding. The sun glinted off his gold fasteners when he dismounted his magnificent stallion. Alex marveled at the pure white destrier horses he and his companion were riding, but behind them was the most beautiful horse Alex had ever seen. It was all black and without a saddle.

"Oy, boy," the man shouted at Alex.

She hurried over. "Yes, sir."

"Do you look after the horses for the innkeeper?"

"Today I do," Alex replied. The nobleman eyed her when Irma arrived at the stable.

"Earl Ainsley, back so soon? I see the sale went well," Irma said as she placed her hand on Alex's shoulder. "And I see you've met my husband's younger brother."

"Thank you, Irma. It went better than I had expected." He looked down at Alex. "So you're one of Ian's brothers. I hear he has a lot of them." Alex smiled and nodded. "I'll make a deal with you, boy. If you take care of my horses, I'll come out after supper and pay you." Irma opened her mouth, but the earl held his hand up. "The Strobels were more than generous. Allow me to share the good fortune."

"Are you up for it, Alex?"

"Naturally," Alex said, pushing her shoulders back and raising her chin.

"Attaboy," the companion said. Dismounting, he handed his horse's reins to Alex before heading inside.

The earl looked Alex over before handing her the horses' reins. "Quick word of warning—watch out for the colt. He'll never take a rider. Too ill-tempered. Even the Strobels said he was hopeless. Don't bother with him. We'll most likely be putting him down when we get back."

Alex opened her mouth but closed it instead.

I'd take a problem horse. They like me.

Taking the reins, Alex nodded to the earl and led the horses into the stable. She directed the colt toward a stall, and he went in with no issue, making her wonder what the nobleman was talking about.

Alex removed the horses' saddles, blankets, and bridles, and she attached a rope to keep them from running off while she fed them oats. Both the nobleman's horses stood still as statues while Alex brushed them. She'd never worked with such well-trained stallions before. After the second one was back in his stall, Alex looked at the colt. He'd remained still while she'd brushed the other horses, but now he was stamping the ground.

Alex crossed her arms and stared at the beast, and to her surprise, he stared back.

"You aren't stubborn and mean, are you? You're just different, and no one understands that."

She walked toward him, and he lowered his head. Alex reached out and stroked his face. The horse let out a soft neigh and turned to look at her.

Fine. I'll take you out, but you better not get me into trouble.

Alex scoffed and then crossed the stable to grab his bridle and lead line. After reattaching them, she led him out the back door into the paddock. She let the horse pull the lead line, and he trotted around the paddock. Alex spoke firmly but kindly, and he began whinnying as he pranced about. Holding his head up high, he looked pleased with himself.

I wonder.

Alex glanced around and, after making sure no one was around, she brought out Irma's saddle. It was too big, but the colt didn't move the entire time she affixed the saddle. Alex stroked his neck and face.

"You're just tired of everyone trying to force you to act a certain way, aren't you? Would you like me to take you for a ride?" She spoke in a soothing tone and continued to stroke him until he was ready to be ridden. Suddenly remembering the earl's words, Alex doubted herself briefly before leading him to the fence. Alex climbed the fence, flung herself on the horse, and a moment later, something deep inside her chest opened. It was like finding a missing piece to complete her soul. The horse responded to her every command as if he could sense it coming. They continued running around the paddock, and just as they were reaching a good speed, a voice rushed past them.

"What in the king's crown is going on here?"

The earl's companion was with Ian, watching her. A wind blew dirt on everyone's faces as Alex tried to swallow her panic. "I'm sorry."

But as she tried to free her foot to dismount, the earl himself appeared. "Stop!" His voice sounded across the paddock. He held up his hand and beckoned her over. Alex swallowed the lump in her throat and marched the horse toward him.

Just then, Irma and Stefan arrived from the inn; the latter's face was beet-red. Alex knew she'd be hearing about this later.

"Who saddled this horse?" the earl asked. He examined the fasteners with narrowed eyes and nodded approvingly.

"I did."

"But you're a child."

"He'll be fourteen next month," Ian chimed in, winking at Alex. "Alex is smart as a whip, especially with horses. It's not his fault he's small in stature."

"You saddled the horse and rode him yourself? With no help from anyone?"

"Yes, sir. I'm sorry if I've acted inappropriately. Dishonoring you wasn't my intention. I finished with your horses, and he seemed impatient, so I thought I'd let him run in the paddock. But he wouldn't leave my side. So I thought I'd try to saddle him, and here I am."

Alex shrugged, then glanced at Stefan, whose lips remained pursed. At least his face wasn't red anymore.

The earl turned toward Irma and Ian. "That colt is almost four, and until today, no one has saddled him, let alone ridden him. I'll make you a trade. The horse for our rooms and food. The Strobels wouldn't take him. He's no use to me now."

Alex couldn't breathe as she looked at Ian and Irma.

"You have a deal, Earl Ainsley," Irma said.

"And it looks like you have a horse, Alex," Ian said. Stefan's mouth dropped open.

"You should close your mouth before the flies get in," Alex said to Stefan, smirking.

The earl and his companion laughed heartily before the earl smiled and shook his head. "You have a gift, young man. When you're older, you and that horse come to Datten. I'll have a job for you in my stables. You can apprentice under my stable master."

"Thank you, sir," Alex replied, and then the group returned to the inn, talking about the dinner menu.

Stefan crossed his arms and rested his foot on the bottom rung of the fence. "Feeling better now?"

"I am. I'm not allowed to kiss who I want, but at least I can go for rides anytime I want to."

"You ride with me or Michael, never alone. Understood?"

"Yes." Alex couldn't help but smile at Stefan. Somehow, her weird talent with horses had come in handy. She had been given a horse *and* saved it from death. Alex stroked his neck and looked him over.

Stefan asked, "Do you have a name in mind?"

"Flash," Alex said. "Because everything important in my life seems to happen in a flash."

THE SPARE WHO BECAME THE HEIR

AARON—SUMMER 1550

As Aaron finished brushing his horse, he could not help but notice that the Warren stable was unusually quiet at this time of day. Was something going on? He quickly dismissed the thought—his mother would have written to Edward that they were coming, and yet no one was here to greet them. Aaron turned to Megesti to see whether he had noticed it too, but the sorcerer was struggling to get his horse to cooperate. Somehow, after sixty-seven years of living in Datten, Megesti still couldn't handle basic horse duties. Aaron had learned them at five and now at twenty, they were instinctual.

Aaron held back a groan. "Just ask Gregory to brush down Sage," he said.

"No," Megesti said. "He always gives me looks when I give him my horse."

"That's because most high-ranking knights from Datten prefer to handle their own horse, whereas yours doesn't even like you."

Megesti glared at Aaron, but Sage took this moment to

stomp on Megesti's foot before rushing for the door. Megesti yelped just as two men appeared. Gregory, the royal stable master, grabbed the horse's bridle. Julius, the youngest son of General Bishop, appeared behind him.

"Welcome to Warren, Your Highness."

"Thank you, Julius. Did my mother warn you of my arrival?" Aaron asked.

"She did."

"Where is General Nial?" Megesti asked. "Isn't he supposed to escort Aaron to see Edward when he arrives?" He surrendered his horse to Gregory.

"The general's detained by a matter of utmost importance at present, so I'm here to collect you and deliver you to my father." Julius motioned for them to follow him.

Aaron and Megesti followed Julius out of the stable and into the large Warren courtyard. The sound of wood striking wood surrounded them, making Aaron smile. In Warren, the young squires trained in the castle courtyard while the senior knights did so in the fields and meadows south of the castle. Aaron laughed before rushing over to a small brown-haired boy. He moved the boy's feet into the correct position and adjusted his grip on the wooden sword. By the time Aaron returned to Julius and Megesti, the boy was laughing, winning his match. Megesti raised his eyebrows but nodded and smiled before Aaron hurried ahead of them into the castle.

Datten was a fortress, always guarded and bursting with knights and warriors, but the castle of Warren bustled with life and citizens. Aaron nodded to everyone as he walked down the beautifully decorated hallway that circled the outside of the primary structure. Even without his crown, he always stood out in Warren. Blond hair was rare here except among Datten-born knights. Even rarer was his gold tunic with the red-and-gold lion crest since Datten knights wore red tunics.

Warren's colors were silver, blue, and green, and their crest depicted two sea dragons holding up a shield emblazoned with a ship. Sea dragons featured prominently in the art that covered the walls, most of which depicted history, lore, and points of pride. Ever since his youth, Aaron's favorite had been the image of the first King and Queen of Warren fighting off the sea dragons. He paused there now while Megesti and Julius caught up.

"Where are we heading?" Aaron asked Julius.

"My father is in General Nial's office."

Aaron leaped to the side as a group of distressed-looking young squires hurried past.

"Just because you're late doesn't mean you can run people over," Julius barked after them.

"Sorry, Sir Bishop," they shouted in unison before rounding the corner. Julius sighed and shook his head as he led Aaron and Megesti toward the general's room.

A knocker shaped like a sea dragon's head adorned the old wooden door. Julius knocked twice, and a deep voice commanded, "Enter." Julius held the door open for the others. Megesti jumped when it banged shut.

Randal's office was always in disarray. The farthest corner contained two enormous bookcases, which always overflowed with journals, scrolls, and papers. The opposite corner featured the general's suit of armor, which he kept on a training dummy, giving the appearance that it watched over him while he worked. In the last corner sat two chairs and a wooden desk that was as large as the military planning table Aaron's father had in Datten. But whereas his father's table was covered in maps and war plans, this one had training schedules and duty rosters. The wall behind the desk held a portrait of the general's family: Randal with his wife, Lady Judith, and their three daughters, Abigail, Diana, and Edith. Aaron had always liked that General Nial had all daughters, and General Bishop had all sons.

Matthew Bishop was examining a large stack of papers on the desk. The Bishops' skin was a warm umber shade, similar to Edward's. An older version of Julius, his graying black hair covered his brown eyes. Aaron waited to be greeted in order to not interrupt his train of thought. Matthew had been a General of Warren since before Aaron was born, and as with General Wafner, Aaron had nothing but respect for him. The man had seen much in his time, including having been the king's general when Princess Victoria was murdered. Many believed his failure to protect the young royals had broken him, allowing General Nial to take his place; but Aaron knew the actual story—that he'd stepped aside to work for Edward and try to learn the truth. Matthew straightened the papers and raised his eyes to meet Aaron's.

"Good afternoon, Your Highness."

"So formal today, Matthew," Aaron teased as he dropped into one of the chairs. "Where's Randal?"

"General Nial had a personal matter to attend to."

Julius snorted, and everyone turned to him.

"Seems like there's a story there," Aaron said with a smirk as he returned his gaze to the general.

Matthew cleared his throat and glared at his son. "As I said, it's a personal matter."

Megesti stood behind the chair beside Aaron. "You look tired, general."

"The old king's illness has progressed. He's agitated and often confused. We find him wandering the halls at night. Some of us suspect he's going mad. It stresses His Royal Highness."

"I'm sorry," Aaron said. "I didn't realize how sick Arthur

had become. Despite everything, that has to be hard on Edward."

Julius snorted again.

"Julius," Matthew warned.

"Is there anything I can do?" Megesti asked. "Now that we're here, I don't think I'll be of much use to Aaron. I'm not good with jousting, so if he intends to train for the fall tournament, there are other noblemen who'd be of more use to him. Perhaps I could assist the royal physician with His Royal Highness."

"Thank you, Megesti," said the general. "We had hoped you would offer. The physician is in the library. We'll have someone bring you something to eat."

"And where's my godfather?" Aaron asked.

"He just finished with the council and is waiting to have dinner with you and Earl Strobel in his room."

"Then I shouldn't keep him waiting." Aaron rose, and the younger men headed toward the door.

Matthew walked around the desk. "Megesti. Julius. Give Aaron and me a minute, please."

Megesti and Julius glanced at Aaron before leaving. As the door closed, the general sighed heavily and leaned on the edge of the desk.

"How is he *really*?"

"Not good. We thought the anniversary last year would be the worst, but this one was so much worse."

"Why are we waiting to find her? Arthur's been dying for years. Even if he caused Victoria's death, what kind of threat can a decrepit old man be?"

"The worry isn't Arthur himself but rather those working for him," Matthew replied. "I'm not convinced he was working alone."

"If that's the case, then how will his death improve

matters?" Aaron asked. "Jerome told me we're waiting until Edward is sure she'll be safe. But if we think he wasn't acting alone, it won't get better even after he's dead."

"We're hoping he's paying people. Mercenaries are expensive, so when the money runs out, they vanish. Jerome and I are also trying to narrow down where to look."

"Any luck?"

Matthew shook his head.

"Is that what has my father in such a foul mood lately?"

"Possibly." Matthew observed him a moment before continuing. "Your mother asked us not to bring it up, so you can expect both your uncle and godfather to."

"Great." Aaron crossed his arms and frowned.

"I shouldn't be saying this, but we're on your side."

"Who's 'we'?" Aaron asked.

"Warren," the general said. "We know the real you and see value in the way you do things."

Aaron smiled.

"Edward's waiting."

Aaron nodded to Matthew, and they headed for the door. Outside, the hallway was empty. The side that housed the royal suites was always more deserted than the front and side hallways. Aaron turned left and walked until he reached Edward's suite; he knocked before opening the door, not waiting to be invited inside.

The first floor of Edward's suite was a meeting room whose walls displayed weapons from former kings of Warren. The wooden table in the center took up most of the space and presently featured a meal of fish, boar, root vegetables, and breads with a few pitchers of ale and some Warren wine. Sitting at the giant table were Edward and Earl Bernhard Strobel. Aaron couldn't help but smile when they looked up at him. Edward's sparkling blue eyes were in stark contrast to his dark brown skin and black hair while Bernhard's blond hair and blue eyes recalled Aaron's mother.

"Aaron," Edward said with a wide smile.

"I wasn't expecting you for a few more weeks," his uncle said.

"Sorry to surprise you, Uncle Bernhard. I needed to get away sooner than expected." Aaron closed the door and took a seat across from them. Grabbing a piece of bread, he watched the two Warren nobles look at each other before turning to him.

His uncle began, "Your mother told me not to mention your arguments with your father—"

"Then maybe you should listen to your older sister," Aaron said before stuffing the bread in his mouth.

"You know you can speak freely with us, Aaron," Edward said. He stood up and poured them each a mug of wine and pushed one toward Aaron before handing another to Bernhard.

Aaron grabbed the mug and held it toward the men before taking a big gulp and setting it down. "Thank you, but I'd rather just joust and work on preparing for the tournament in September. The only time my father seems to care is when I win." Aaron turned to his uncle. "Is Cam ready to be knocked off his horse a lot this week?"

"He's escorting his mother to pick up some older relatives."

"Marco Bishop joined them," Edward added.

"I've missed something," Aaron said as he finished filling his plate with food. "What is going on with the Nials and Bishops?"

"There is to be a wedding in two weeks," Bernhard said. "The Nial's oldest daughter, Abigail, will marry the middle Bishop boy, Aiden."

"A Bishop and a Nial?" Aaron asked.

"Yes." Edward smiled.

"But why is Aunt Elfrieda going?"

"A great deal goes into planning a wedding, especially on short notice and with such prestigious families involved," Bernhard said.

"Knowing how busy Judith and Lillian are, planning everything, Elfrieda volunteered to fetch the older relatives from the smaller towns. I tried to insist she take some men with her, but she was happy with Cam and Marco. Julius is staying here, so you'll have the youngest Bishop and Nial to keep you company."

"Isn't Edith busy helping with her sister's wedding?" Aaron asked.

Edward chuckled. "I think Randal and Judith find having Edith out of the way is more helpful. Julius has been keeping her occupied."

"I noticed. Julius snorted anytime we mentioned the Nials." Aaron narrowed his eyes when he noticed Edward and Bernhard had gone quiet. "Someone caught them, didn't they?"

Edward's head snapped up. "You knew too?"

Aaron smiled before taking another gulp of wine. "I'm observant. You know that."

"Yet you said nothing? So much for Datten honor." Bernhard winked at Edward, making Aaron roll his eyes.

His uncle enjoyed taunting Datten's legacy. Aaron understood; it had never thrilled Bernhard that Guinevere married Emmerich. More than once he'd told Aaron the only good things that came out of that marriage had been him and his brother.

"Everyone could see that Abigail and Aiden had feelings for each other," Aaron said, pointing his fork at his uncle before he took another bite of his boar.

"They've been inseparable for most of their lives. Frankly, I had expected the generals to announce an engagement years ago," Edward said.

"I still remember when I was little, Mother joked about them marrying almost as much as she did about me and ..." Aaron's throat went dry.

"Elizabeth," Bernhard finished for him. "More ludicrous logic from the great King of Datten. See your son befriend a beautiful princess, so betroth her to his brother."

"Bernhard." Edward's tone was gruff and sharp. "I won't have you belittling Emmerich in front of Aaron. He has a reason for everything he does, even if he won't tell us."

"Apologizes, Your Royal Highness—I forgot my place."

"I appreciate your honesty, Bernhard. I always have," Edward said. "But I also think Aaron has enough issues with his father without adding yours. No one forced your sister into her marriage. She met Emmerich by chance at a feast my father threw in his honor after his first major victory against the Betruger."

"I remember," Bernhard said before he chugged the last of the wine.

"Good. Because I do too, and I was only a boy. Guinevere took his breath away."

"And then he took her voice away," Bernhard grumbled.

"No, he didn't," Aaron said. Bernhard turned to him, but Aaron's eyes were on Edward.

He shrugged at Aaron. "Your choice, Aaron."

"What's your choice?" Bernhard asked.

Aaron sighed. "Whether or not to tell you the truth about what goes on in Datten. My mother plays the devoted, demure Queen of Datten role so well, everyone believes it. Everyone except the Wafners, Edward, and me."

"Explain."

"For as long as I can remember, my mother has never kept

silent when my father displeases her. He may not do what she says, but he hears her out. They just know what's expected of our people. So the feisty, opinionated sister you loved is still there—she's just more selective of who she shares her thoughts with." Aaron smiled as he finished, stuffing a giant piece of boar into his mouth.

"Is this true, Edward?"

"It is."

"Then why did no one tell me all these years?"

"It wouldn't have changed your mind," Aaron said. "You never liked Datten or what they stood for. It doesn't matter how well my father treats my mother. It will always upset you that she left Warren."

Bernhard stared at Aaron. "You're too smart for your own good."

Aaron smiled at his uncle and shrugged. "I watch people. I like to know what makes people do what they do."

"There's that curious Strobel blood." Edward nodded, raising his glass.

"Council went long today. What was so interesting?" Aaron asked.

"My father," Edward said. "He's not well, and he's causing problems."

"Problems how?"

"He wakes up at night and has gotten away from his physician a few times. Knights have found him wandering the halls muttering to himself."

"So we wanted you to know you are welcome to stay at the estate, if you prefer. With His Royal Highness's illness keeping him from sleep, he's been on a warpath."

"Thank you, Bernhard, but I'd prefer to stay in my usual room at the castle. After all these years, I'm good at avoiding Arthur. It shouldn't be a problem."

"So what was the fight about this time?" Edward asked, looking Aaron over more carefully than he liked.

"The usual."

Bernhard smiled at them. "I think this is where I leave you so you can talk to Edward alone. Future king to acting king and all that. Come by the estate tomorrow when you wake up. Bring the youngest Bishop and Nial with you, and we'll see how jousting goes."

"Julius volunteered." Edward grinned.

"Delightful. I have beaten both of his older brothers at tournaments. I suspect the youngest Bishop is trying to find my weakness before next month's tournament."

"He is Matthew's son," Bernhard replied, smiling.

"Too bad for him. I don't have a weakness when I'm on my horse. On my feet, I have many, but on Thunder, nothing distracts me."

"And there's the Datten arrogance," Bernhard said, ruffling Aaron's hair before bowing to Edward and leaving.

"Now, the truth. Why did you run?" Edward asked once the door closed.

"He expects me to be my brother. We both know I never will be, no matter how much I train with Jerome. He wants me to be skilled in battle and capable of leading a cavalry, but any time I ask for a chance, he denies me."

"I suspect it's your mother that's keeping you out of harm's way."

Aaron sighed, pushing his plate away.

"I have a proposal, Your Highness," Edward said. "Why don't you take over the knight training while you're here? Randal and Matthew are busy with the wedding, so it would help them. Most of the men are from Datten, so they should listen to you, provided Matthew tells them you're in charge."

"You mean it?"

Edward smiled. "I know what it's like to stand in the long shadow of an intimidating king and feel you'll never measure up."

"Thank you."

"Don't thank me yet. There are some knights who won't enjoy being ordered around by a young prince. You can start the day after tomorrow. I'll let the generals know tomorrow at the daily briefing."

"I'll be ready." Aaron stood. "If you'll excuse me, I'm going to grab some books from the library and head up to my room to review them."

Edward nodded, and Aaron bowed and left the room. Aaron found a few training books on the royal military shelves of the library. Satisfied, he grabbed a torch and thrust it into the fire. Tucking the books under his arm, he pulled open the painting on the library's second floor using a secret lever and revealed a dank, narrow tunnel. He entered the secret passage, closed the portrait behind him, and headed for his bedroom. Aaron passed an empty royal suite and Daniel's untouched room before arriving at his own.

The fireplace was already lit, making Aaron smile. Edward had known he would stay at the castle, even with his uncle's offer. Edward understood Aaron's internal struggles better than anyone—both the desire to make his kingdom proud in his own way while also craving his father's approval.

The furniture in Aaron's room was sparse but luxurious. Edward ensured they covered the four-poster bed with a Datten quilt despite being in Warren. On the other side of the room, he'd filled the wardrobe with Warren and Datten tunics. Some were the simple kind worn by knights; others were reserved for nobles, and of course, there was a pair of royal Datten tunics that only Aaron's family could wear. Aaron stripped off his dirty clothes and threw on a pair of clean sleeping pants. The table beside the wardrobe held his traveling satchel, but he let it sit.

Aaron pulled his copy of *The Iliad* off his small bookshelf and tossed it on the bed. It had been his favorite ever since Daniel had read it to him as a boy. He had so many memories of going off on adventures in the woods of Datten. When they visited Warren, Elizabeth always wanted Daniel to read it to her too, and he had obliged her. The young Princess Elizabeth had bewitched Aaron and Daniel almost as easily as she had Edward.

What would they be like today?

Aaron fell asleep dreaming of them.

Aaron woke early and was dressed in his training clothes before the sun rose. Morning dew had soaked his feet since the start of his normal morning ten-mile run, and goose bumps covered his arms as he ran harder. Even without Jerome to order him around, Aaron knew he must continue his training while in Warren or else suffer upon his return. After the run, he washed up and hurried to the dining hall before the knights could eat everything. Edward and Megesti weren't there, but Aaron had expected that. After learning what was going on with Arthur, he assumed they would have been up with him until late.

Aaron spotted Julius while leaving the dining hall.

"Good morning, Prince Aaron." The youngest Bishop bowed, and Aaron chuckled as a sweet voice sounded behind him.

"Good morning, Your Highness. I hear we're to keep you company today."

Aaron turned to face Edith. General Nial's youngest daughter was the most memorable of the girls. Her figure allowed her to fit into any dress her mother chose, but she also possessed a strength her sisters could never match. Despite being the palest of the Nials, her sand-colored skin sparkled like Warren's beaches and told everyone who her father was. She wore her raven-black hair in a simple braid, and her brown eyes sparkled like her father's. Randal's and Edith's eyes reminded Aaron of wet sand, and he often wondered what was going on beneath them.

"You know you're supposed to call me Aaron."

Edith laughed a little too loudly and looped her arm through Julius's. "Not when my father is around the corner."

Aaron nodded and cleared his throat. "We're off, Randal. Thank you for bringing Edith."

Footsteps echoed in the hallway as the general rounded the corner. Randal's hair was a mess, and his eyes were duller than Aaron had ever seen. Even his usually impeccable uniform was askew—Aaron couldn't think of a time he looked worse.

"Thank you, Your Highness. Megesti is already waiting at the stables." Randal bowed to Aaron before turning to Edith and Julius. "Behave." Then he hurried down the hall past the king's room.

"What was that about?" Aaron asked.

"Things have gotten even more interesting for the wedding planning," Julius said as the trio headed down the hall toward the stables.

"Oh?" Aaron asked, turning to Edith, who was grinning from ear to ear.

"I'm going to be an aunt."

Aaron sucked his breath through his teeth. "Poor Randal and Matthew. Two generals who couldn't keep track of their own children. That has to hurt their reputations."

"Which is why the wedding is being rushed even more now," Julius said.

They soon arrived at the stables. Megesti had asked the stable boys to prepare horses for them, and soon they were off.

The ride to the Strobel estate was short, especially since Aaron raced Edith and Julius there. Their horses cantered down the main road, taking them past both the Bishop and Nial estates, and the three of them were eager to do this unnoticed. The estates of the Warren nobility were massive, and the land owned by them often was so plentiful that they lived in town and hired farmers to tend to it.

At the end of the street stood another grand manor, a cobblestone path leading from the road to the guest stables. The house's decorations were impeccable but still welcoming in a way the others on the street couldn't manage. The air smelled of fresh hay, and Aaron could see his uncle out at the paddock already.

"Morning, Uncle Bernhard," Aaron shouted as they approached the stables.

"Good morning, Aaron. Hello, Julius, Edith. I trust you're excited about the upcoming wedding."

"Very," Edith said with a mischievous glint in her eyes. Julius dismounted and grabbed Edith's horse for her to dismount. Almost immediately, a stable boy was at her side, ready to take the horse.

"Take Buttercup to the mares' stable, Fredrick," Bernhard said, and the boy nodded before heading off.

"How do you remember every horse's name?" Aaron asked, dismounting so fast his uncle shook his head.

"The same way you remember all the Datten knights' names. What would you like to work on today? Speed? Agility? Balance?"

Aaron examined Julius. *You'll be a good opponent. You're from Warren and know horses. Plus, being a general's son, you should have some tricks.*

"Let's let Julius pick. What is your strength, Julius?" Aaron smirked at his friend in the Warren knight shirt while adjusting his matching tunic.

Edith laughed, looking from Julius to Aaron and back. "This should be entertaining."

"I believe you're right, Edith. Should I ask the stable boys to fetch you a bench?" Bernhard asked.

"If you promise not to tell my mother, I'm fine sitting on the fence," Edith said, still eyeing the men before her.

"It'll be our secret. So, *boys*, what will it be?"

"Sword work first, then speed. I find it's more challenging to aim the lance after sparring first," Julius said.

Aaron nodded and handed his horse to the stable boy, who'd returned. "You can leave the saddle on, but he'll want some water. We'll finish with our sparring sooner than Sir Bishop expects."

Julius's laugh filled the field as Aaron moved past the paddocks toward the jousting and sparring area. He couldn't help but smile at Julius's confidence. Aaron knew Matthew and his brother would have made sure he was ready for anything, but Matthew wasn't Jerome. And Julius's brothers, Marco and Aiden, hadn't followed their father into knighthood, so they were not on the same level as the Datten royal guard Aaron trained with. Aaron and Julius eyed one another as they arrived at the circle and drew their blades.

"Oh no you don't," Bernhard said. "I don't care how much you've practiced, you are not using steel on my watch. I don't want to explain to the generals or Edward why one of you needed stitches."

Edith giggled. "I thought you'd be more worried about Elfrieda. Julius is her blood nephew, just as Aaron is yours. If she's anything like my mother, she'd have more than your head if they got hurt."

"Quite perceptive, Lady Edith," Bernhard said, laughing. "All right, boys, grab a sword from the barrel by the trough."

Aaron pulled out a half dozen swords and held them out to Julius so he could choose first. Julius examined each for length and straightness before selecting one.

Not checking the balance or handle grip?

Aaron checked a few swords, then selected the one whose grip fit his hand perfectly and whose wood was in perfect condition. Slicing through the air, Aaron walked after Julius and took his place in the circle.

Datten tradition required that they bow to one another and show their swords. Despite being Warren born, Julius had trained in Datten for several years—the best knights always did eventually. Aaron watched Julius take his place, noting his preference for his left leg.

"You're so quiet, Aaron," Julius said. "I always thought Datten men boasted more."

A sudden breeze sent everyone's tunics flapping. Aaron smiled, knowing Julius was trying to bait him. "If you were actually competition, I'd be boasting."

Edith's laugh rang out, and all the men turned to her. Julius's expression soured for a moment before Bernhard spoke up.

"Don't scold her, Julius. You started the verbal sparring, but Aaron finished it. Be careful with him. He's the most dangerous combination of Warren and Datten."

"You sound like my father, but he means it differently," Aaron said. He pointed his sword at Julius. "Come on, Warren, let's see what you're made of."

Julius raised his sword with half a smile. "You're only confident because you beat my brothers, but you forget I trained better."

"Yes, you're both trained by a general. We get it. Start fighting already," Edith said, making Bernhard laugh.

"You heard the lady!"

Aaron kept his eyes fixed on Julius as he turned toward Edith and Bernhard. Julius fell for the ruse and lunged at Aaron. He dodged to the left, sending Julius stumbling toward the ground. Dust swirled about them as Julius caught himself. Adding further insult, Aaron kicked him in the rear, laughing. Steadying himself, Julius spun the wooden sword in his hand and pointed it at Aaron.

Aaron bowed to Julius, mocking him, and the knight quickly stalked toward him. Aaron gave him access to his favored leg. His father had trained Julius the same way as all the Datten knights, but Aaron could outmaneuver every action the generals had taught them. He ducked Julius's large swing and then cracked his sword on Julius's hip. Edith gasped, but Julius wasted no time spinning to face Aaron, who shifted his stance to put more weight behind his swing and quickly struck Julius hard on the thigh.

Julius's yelp gave Aaron pause. "Do you yield, Sir Bishop?"

"No." Julius wiped his hand on his pants before taking up his sword once more.

Looking his friend over, Aaron decided how many rounds he'd wear Julius down before finishing this.

After another twenty minutes and three rounds, Julius's chest was heaving, but Aaron hadn't even broken a sweat. Jerome's commanding voice resounded in Aaron's mind as he watched Julius shuffle around the ring. Aaron bounced on the balls of his feet as he waited. Daniel took after their father in terms of size and strength, but Aaron had gotten his father's speed. Julius's next move was the one Aaron had been waiting for. Aaron took his sword in both hands and lunged at Julius with lightning speed, bringing his sword down onto Julius's between the blade and the guard. As Aaron expected, the wooden sword broke in two.

"*Now* I yield," Julius said, examining his broken sword. "What did I forget?"

"You didn't inspect it all over or check the balance."

Julius groaned and nodded.

"Jousting next?" Edith asked.

Aaron smiled. Jousting was his best event, and he ended up knocking Julius off his horse three times in five runs before Bernhard stepped in. After the final fall, Aaron dismounted and helped Julius up. A stable boy took the horses to get them some water.

"Okay, that's enough for today," Bernhard said. "You did well, Julius."

Julius slapped his pants to clean himself off as best he could while Aaron straightened his tunic and smiled at Edith as she headed over.

"You're all welcome to stay for lunch," Bernhard offered.

"Thank you, earl, but we're expected to help my mother this afternoon with wedding preparations," Edith said, sighing.

"Edith is expected to help, and I'm expected to keep her on task." Julius laughed, kicking dirt at her.

"You sure?" Aaron asked. "We could tell your fathers I insisted."

"Thank you, but they left me out of a lot of the planning because my sister doesn't think I'm ladylike enough for the tasks. So if she's found something for me to do, I'd like to help."

"And if Edith has to go somewhere, I'm responsible for her safety while her father is busy, so I'll be escorting her around Warren."

"With you at her side so much, is it any wonder he can't find her a suitable match?" Bernhard asked.

"I'm only eighteen. I have time." Edith's face fell as she looked from Julius to Bernhard.

"You're by far the most beautiful of the Nial daughters. You should have been spoken for years ago, but your vivacious nature, combined with how much time you spend with Julius, makes noblemen nervous around you."

Edith cocked her head to the side and bit her lip.

"I request you speak your mind, Lady Edith." Aaron bowed to her in the same dramatic way he'd done that morning.

Edith held her chin up and shook her head hard enough to send her braid bouncing on her back. "If a man can't handle my exuberance, then he's not worthy of me."

"And the rest?" Aaron asked. He crossed his arms at Edith, making Julius smirk.

Blushing, she turned to Bernhard. "Seeing as your own son is twenty-three and has yet to have a serious prospect, perhaps you shouldn't judge."

Aaron and Julius burst into laughter. Bernhard clapped his hands and smiled at Edith. "Spoken like your father, dear. Poor Randal. No man is ever going to live up to the expectations he has for your future husband."

"On that note, I think we should head home," Julius said. He moved behind Edith and playfully pushed her. In retaliation, she swiped her head to the side, sending her braid into Julius's face and making him cry out.

"Thank you, Bernhard." Edith curtsied to him and Aaron despite being in pants.

Bernhard bowed in return while Aaron nodded. Edith and Julius headed toward the stable, and once they reached it, Aaron turned to his uncle.

"What's for lunch?"

"Boar," Bernhard said, patting Aaron on the shoulder and

turning him toward the house. "Now let's talk about why you fled from Datten."

"I didn't *flee*," Aaron objected. "And I'm certain my mother told you not to ask about it."

"She did. But she's not here, and if your father is being hard on you again, I want to know so I can give him a piece of my mind when he comes to the wedding."

"They're coming?"

"Of course. The daughter of a Warren general is marrying the son of the other Warren general. We're uniting two of the oldest Warren families. It's an important occasion."

"Don't," Aaron said, stepping ahead of his uncle.

"Don't what? Say that the only wedding that will excite Warren more is the one of the crown princess? If she ever comes home, and they decide to follow tradition—"

Aaron spun around to face his uncle. "If you want me to stay for lunch, we're *not* discussing this."

Bernhard chuckled and spun Aaron back toward the manor. "Fine. We'll talk about my handsome son. Have you seen any ladies that may catch his eye?"

Aaron laughed and rolled his eyes.

WHEN HE ARRIVED BACK at the castle, Aaron headed to his room to read before dinner. Unpacking his bag, he placed his crown on the table and pulled his books out to put on the bookshelf. Before he could, however, a loud crash sounded from the other side of his wall. Aaron rushed out the door and down the narrow hallway, almost slipping on a piece of armor that went skittering across the stone floor. Aaron kicked it aside and looked up to see King Arthur muttering in the hallway.

Wearing only a nightshirt, he was rubbing his arms and shaking.

"Your Royal Highness?" Aaron moved toward the king.

Arthur stopped muttering and slowly turned to Aaron. His forehead glistened, and his eyes appeared hollow and sunken. Aaron couldn't believe the difference from the last time he'd seen him a few months ago—he'd aged a decade in that time, but the rage in his eyes was the same. He always looked angry with everyone.

"It was supposed to be you. I heard her tell him, but I won't allow that. I will not give him the satisfaction. Not after what that whore did, and she'll be the same. You'll see. Even Datten can't change that."

"Arthur, you're tired and confused. Let's get you back to your room." Aaron moved to take Arthur's arm, but despite the illness, he was as strong as ever. Pain flooded Aaron's arm and shoulder as the old king twisted his forearm and slammed him into the wall.

"They won't find it. No one is getting my sword. It's still red. I never cleaned it and won't until my line ends. I'll burn before they find it. Your treacherous father played his part. Oh, he did, and he paid. Everyone paid ... or they will."

Trying to hide his discomfort, Aaron spoke gently. "Well, I can promise you no one wants your rusted old sword, so let's get you back to bed."

Arthur's eyes locked onto Aaron's as a low growl left the king. He glared at Aaron another moment before releasing him slowly.

"You have Warren in you, boy. I can see it," Arthur said before he went back to muttering. Footsteps sounded down the hallway, getting louder.

"Prince Aaron." Warren's royal physician sighed at finding

them together. "Thank you for finding him. I've been looking for His Royal Highness for an hour."

"Of course. Do you need help to get him back to his room?"

"*I'll* help."

Aaron looked over his shoulder to see Edward coming down the hall.

"You had a busy morning and need to prepare for tomorrow." His godfather patted Aaron on the back as they looked at the old king. Edward sighed loudly. The air between them became heavy as the physician guided Arthur down the hall.

"Did he say anything to you? He hasn't spoken to anyone in months."

Eyes wide, Aaron turned to Edward and nodded. "Some nonsense about his sword, Datten, and me having too much Warren. He sounded an awful lot like my father. Nothing meaningful, if that's what you were hoping."

With a last pat on the back, Edward walked after his father while Aaron remained absolutely still, puzzling over what he'd just experienced.

THE ADVENTURE BEGINS

AARON—WINTER 1552

Prince Aaron made his way across the crowded training field. It was still dark out, and his legs were burning from the ten-mile run with the elite guard.

Avery Reinhart, the king's archery general, was waiting for him. "The king demands an audience, Your Highness."

Aaron paused and looked Avery up and down. "Now? I just finished the run."

All around him, young boys hoping to one day become knights sparred with each other. The kingdom of Datten, founded over fifteen hundred years ago, trained most of the knights across all of Torian.

The general cleared his throat, bringing Aaron's attention back to him. "Your mother and father are already waiting in the throne room."

Aaron sighed and headed toward the castle. The snow crunched beneath his boots as he strode along the path and into the torchlit courtyard. Nothing was more important to Aaron's battle-hardened father than training. Aaron struggled to think what he'd done recently that would make his father angry enough to pull him out of it. Last night, he'd woken up to a commotion coming from the floor below his bedroom, but he had ignored it and gone back to sleep.

Aaron took the smaller side stairs leading out of the court-yard. Built for the servants and knights to slip in unnoticed, Aaron preferred them to the ostentatious front entrance stairs. His father hated it when he used them, stating it implied Aaron was behaving beneath his station or simply lazy as the servants' stairs came out close to his bedroom tower. In reality, Aaron could never take the front stairs without being reminded of the duty and responsibility that awaited him should be become king after his father. The main stairs were unchanged since Datten's founding, and each step made Aaron think of all the brilliant kings who walked them before him. The smaller steps allowed him to feel at one with their people, a skill he felt his father lacked. He hurried up the last steps and turned down the large main hallway. It was early enough that not even the servants were around yet. Aaron nodded to the few knights on duty and rounded the corner toward the throne room.

To show off Datten's prosperity, they had elaborately deco-rated the main hall. Paintings of famous battles and historical events lined the walls. Tables covered in statues and trinkets gifted by other kingdoms over the centuries lined the entrance, and suits of armor from former kings stood guard around the entrance doors to the throne room and dining hall. Aaron paused at the smallest one—this suit of armor belonged to the king who would never be.

Aaron looked up and sighed. The massive wooden throne room doors were only closed when the meeting was of the utmost secrecy. He took a deep breath and knocked.

"Enter!" his father ordered.

Aaron pushed open the doors and did a double take. On the

usually bare stone wall behind the thrones now hung the old painting of the kingdom of Warren's royalty, the portrait that had been in Merlock and Megesti's lab for years. In the painting, Prince Edward's dark skin, black hair, and blue eyes were the polar opposite of his wife and daughter. There was no mistaking Victoria and Elizabeth as mother and daughter, even when Elizabeth was only four. Both shared the same wild, wavy chestnut locks and emerald-green eyes.

His footsteps echoed through the hall as he strutted toward the royals with his head held high. He couldn't stop looking at the painting.

Are you scowling at me, Elizabeth?

Despite the hour, the queen had dressed in a fiery red gown made of the finest silk. His mother stood in front of the obsidian stone dais that held their thrones. Her hand rested on his father's shoulder, something she only did if nervous about what his father might do.

King Emmerich stood as if ready to lead the Datten army into battle. Aaron wiped his clammy hands on his pants as he continued walking toward his parents. Their graying golden hair gleamed in the glow of the torches, but neither of them moved. Their stoic expressions made his stomach twist, and when he reached them, Aaron bowed even though he didn't have to. Datten's king and queen commanded respect, but they had never required him to bow to them.

"General Reinhart mentioned you wished to see me," Aaron said.

"Yes, but we want to wait for the others before we give you your orders," Emmerich said.

"Others?" Aaron looked around, confused. "Orders?"

As if on cue, the hall's side door opened, revealing General Wafner, his father's most trusted advisor and Torian's fiercest warrior. He'd been Aaron and Daniel's teacher since boyhood.

Today, Jerome was dressed like a simple peasant and not the general of the most powerful kingdom in Torian. Megesti followed him into the room. The sorcerer spotted the painting too. Giving Aaron a look, he tilted his head toward it, but Aaron shrugged.

"Your Royal Highnesses, we're here as requested," Jerome said, taking a knee.

Aaron exchanged a wide-eyed look with Megesti. Jerome had no reason to be so formal with them either.

What is happening?

A loud crack echoed through the hall, and Merlock appeared with Edward at his side. Aaron smiled, but Edward's posture was off, and his clothes were strange. It took Aaron a moment to realize his godfather was in his sleeping clothes. Edward looked around the room and raced toward Emmerich. Merlock merely sighed and trudged after him.

Aaron retreated from the throne until he reached Merlock, and then they backed away while the senior royals conferred privately. Aaron couldn't make out Edward's words, but his anxious tone was clear. He grabbed Emmerich and shook him, an action Aaron had never seen him do. Emmerich's face went pale as he looked at Aaron and then turned to Jerome and Megesti.

"Fine," Emmerich snapped.

Aaron looked at his mother. Her hand was at her neck, and she had tears in her eyes. She shook her head at his father and tried to grab his arm, but Emmerich was too quick. Her lip quivered as she watched him approach Jerome.

"Jerome. Megesti. I assume you know why we summoned you," Emmerich said, and they both nodded.

"I don't," Aaron said, stepping forward.

"He's dying," Edward said, his voice hollow.

"Who's dying?" Aaron asked.

"My father," Edward said. He took a seat on the dais stairs, holding his head in his hands, his elbows propped up on his knees.

"Dying? Hasn't Arthur been dying for years?"

They'd been down this road before. With his health declining, the old King of Warren had conceded and begrudgingly gave the running of the kingdom to Edward years ago.

"He's beyond even my help now." Merlock rubbed his hands and moved toward his son. Megesti stood tall as his father patted his shoulder.

"My father won't be able to hold on much longer. He's sixty-eight, for goodness' sake. It's time. I've waited fourteen years already. I want her home."

Her.

"You mean Elizabeth," Aaron said. "We're being sent to find the lost Princess of Warren, aren't we?"

"You and Megesti are being sent to find her," Emmerich said. "Jerome will go to protect you."

"A larger party would be too noticeable. If someone has her, they might run," Edward said.

"Megesti and Elizabeth are blood," Merlock said. "He can sense blood kin better than any sorcerer I've ever met. Assuming she has any sort of power, you will only need to be in the correct village or town, and he'll know she's there."

"So he can locate his own bloodline the way a hunting dog detects prey?" Jerome asked.

Aaron chuckled at the idea of his best friend being compared to a dog. Then a terrible thought hit him.

"What if she isn't what we expect?" Aaron asked.

"What do you mean?" Guinevere asked.

"She's eighteen. What if she's married? What if she was being held against her will all this time?"

Edward's shoulders sagged, and his face paled. Aaron

suspected he was considering the implications. Breathing out, he patted his knees before turning to Aaron.

"That's the other reason Jerome is going. I don't care where you find her or what she is. You bring my daughter back to me. She is the Crown Princess of Warren. If she's married—or worse—we'll handle it when she's back safe," Edward said.

"If her husband is unsuitable, we could arrange an accident. That would solve the problem," Emmerich said.

"Emmerich!" His mother slapped his father's shoulder.

Aaron tried to hide his glee. "You're trusting me with such an important job?"

"I'm not," Emmerich said. "I don't trust you with anything."

"I am," Edward said, pushing himself to his feet. He strode past Emmerich to Aaron. "You spent more time with Elizabeth than I did before she vanished. The only people alive with a chance of finding her are in this room, and we can't send your mother."

"Why isn't Merlock coming?" Aaron asked.

"If I were to vanish, it would raise questions. But you and Megesti heading off on a journey is understandable, especially for a prince trying to prove himself to his stubborn father," Merlock said.

Emmerich cleared his throat and stared down his sorcerer.

"With all due respect to Your Royal Highness, all of Torian is aware of your stubborn streak and your disagreements with Aaron," Merlock said.

"What's the plan?" Jerome asked. "We go from town to town waiting for Megesti to sense her and then look for a younger version of Victoria?"

"No. She won't look like her mother when you find her," Merlock said.

"What do you mean?" Emmerich asked, pointing at the

painting on the wall. "We all have eyes. Elizabeth looks nothing like Edward."

"When Elizabeth was born, I gifted Victoria a necklace, one of the few things I brought from the Forbidden Lands. It belonged to our mother, and it hid her when her role as her generation's most gifted healer became too much for her. After my sister's death, I looked for it but couldn't find the necklace. Today, I learned from Edward that Elizabeth was wearing it the day she vanished. Victoria must have done something to it to make it not function that day. If Elizabeth still has it, she won't look like herself. Except for the eyes."

"How much not like herself?" Aaron asked.

"She'll appear as a boy," Merlock replied.

"You're right. When she hid with us, she looked more boy than girl," Jerome said.

"But it bodes well for the hope that she survived," Edward said. "I know it's been fourteen years and we haven't heard a whisper, but I haven't given up hope."

He looked at Emmerich. A sadness passed over their eyes, and Aaron knew they were remembering the anniversary of when someone had murdered Edward's cousin, and Edward had tried to take his own life.

Father, thank you for forcing your way into Edward's room and saving him. I can't imagine my life without my godfather.

Aaron raised his eyebrows at Megesti, and he smiled back.

"It'll take time, but we can do this," Aaron said.

"I agree with Aaron," Jerome said. "Don't worry, Your Majesty. I'll make sure our prince comes home."

Aaron swallowed as his mother looked at Emmerich and then at Aaron.

"We will succeed, Mother. I'll be fine," Aaron said.

"You'd better," Emmerich said.

Typical.

Aaron crossed his arms and glared at his father. "Doubting my abilities before I've even left? Where's the honor in that?"

"If you think asking Jerome to start training you five years ago would be enough to earn my respect, you're delusional. It isn't good enough. You aren't trying hard enough. Everyone knows about your soft heart. You're your mother's son and always have been."

"Just say what you really think," Aaron said. "I'm not good enough for you and never will be. I have spent my entire life trying to live up to a dead prince's memory."

As soon as the words left his mouth, Aaron regretted them. He knew the pained expression on his mother's face at the mention of his brother would haunt him for a long time. Unfortunately, he was so fixated on his mother that he never saw his father coming. Emmerich grabbed him by the front of his shirt and dragged him forward so hard he bit his lip.

"Never speak of your brother with such disrespect!" Emmerich shouted at him.

Adrenaline rushed through Aaron as he shoved his father away. Emmerich tried to grab him again, but Aaron dodged him. He looked up at his father and wiped the blood from his lip.

There were three things he'd gotten from his father: his blond hair, his tactical planning, and his temper. The last one Aaron hid well, but he knew that twitching vein on his father's face. Their Datten tempers raged through them, but before Aaron could retaliate, Jerome and Edward rushed from their spots and kept them apart.

"Emmerich! Aaron!" his mother screamed, leaving her spot. "Stop it, both of you."

"Mark my words, you have miles to go if you want to earn my crown, *young man*."

"If having your crown means being compared to you, I

don't want it." Trying to calm his breathing, Aaron looked from Jerome to Megesti.

"We should leave today," Megesti suggested.

"Pack light. We can leave once we're done." Aaron turned to Edward. "If she's out there, we'll bring her back."

"Do General Bishop or Nial have any ideas?" Jerome asked.

"General Bishop believes she's in northern Datten, somewhere in the Dark Forest, or even at the beginning of the Ogre Mountain range."

"Then we'll start there. No one knows who we are," Jerome said.

Aaron nodded to Jerome and Edward, then tried to reassure his mother with a soft smile. Looking at his father, he swallowed his rage and stormed out. As soon as he reached the hallway, Aaron grabbed the first vase he found and threw it against the wall, barely missing Megesti, who'd followed him. The vase shattered, sending pieces flying everywhere.

Megesti sighed. "I see you are taking your disagreement well." He adjusted his cloak, and when he looked up, he gasped. "Aaron, you're bleeding."

Don't take it out on him.

"I'll be fine. You know he gets to me."

"I had hoped the conversation would have gone better, but it could have gone worse too. The only person in that room who doesn't think we can do this is your father, and His Royal Highness is most likely terrified of something happening to you."

"No, he isn't. He probably wishes I were the royal who vanished instead of Elizabeth."

Megesti squeezed Aaron's shoulder. "That isn't true. I found you with Jerome. The relief on your father's face when you were safe was obvious. I've known your father his entire life."

Aaron snorted. "I suppose it's even more frustrating for you."

"Oh?"

"You grew up with him. He should know what you are capable of."

"That's the trouble with mortals. So forgetful," Megesti said, smirking.

Aaron shook his head. "Don't pack your entire library. We need to pass as peasants."

"Understood."

A loud crack came from the throne room.

"Looks like my father is taking King Edward back to Warren before anyone realizes he's gone."

"Good. Who knows what Arthur could manage if he got wind of this?" Aaron said as they headed in opposite directions toward the towers that housed their bedrooms.

Aaron didn't bother to remove his training clothes as dirty seemed like an appropriate way to start a journey where he'd need to hide his royal station. Aaron threw his satchel and saddlebag on his bed before he opened his wardrobe. He packed the oldest training clothes he owned—high quality but worn. Winter in the castle was difficult, but the storms where the mountains hit the Dark Forest would be much worse. Glancing at his cloaks, Aaron grabbed a riding one. He didn't own any simple ones, but at least this one didn't feature his crest; instead, it was lined with glittering gold material.

The horizon over the forest was already lightening. Aaron guessed Megesti would be deciding between books and possibly forgetting to pack spare clothes. Shaking his head, Aaron paused at his own bookshelf. Packing smart was critical, so only two books would come with him. *Plants of the Dark Forest* had saved his life during the honor rite when he was traveling through the forest to get home, so he picked that one.

And since myths and legends were a favorite of his and Daniel's in their youth and since this pristine copy was the last thing Daniel had gifted him, he selected *The Iliad* as well. Tucking both books into his satchel, Aaron grabbed his sword and belt off the table beside his bed.

Aaron turned when he heard footsteps echoing up the stairs. When his mother appeared, her eyes were red and her lips a slit. Aaron recognized that look.

Stepping away from his packing, he took her hands in his. "I'll be fine, Mother. I promise we'll be careful."

Her breath hitched as she pulled her hand from Aaron's and placed it on his cheek. The last few years, he'd grown so much that his mother now had to raise her hand to caress his cheek.

"Your father is right, Aaron. You were always mine, and Daniel was his. I need you to find her and come home. Losing your brother nearly broke me, but losing you ... would kill me."

Aaron smiled down at her. "I promise. I'll come back, and everything will be fine, and life will go back to normal."

Guinevere smiled. "It won't be, dear. When you find Elizabeth, nothing will ever be the same again. Not for Warren, Datten, or Torian, and that's okay. It's time. You couldn't stay mine forever."

"What do you mean?" Aaron asked, but Guinevere kissed his other cheek before releasing his face.

"You'll see, dear."

Guinevere loosened her belt, pulled out a small bag, and handed it to him.

Opening the bag, Aaron saw that she had filled it with gold coins. "Mother?"

The smile that spread across her face was one he loved. Her eyes even twinkled.

"I know you secretly help those less fortunate, especially

in the small villages. You've had a passion for helping the poor in our kingdom ever since you returned from your honor rite, and while your father has no interest in nurturing it, I do. Give this to whomever you think needs it and deserves it."

"Won't he be angry?"

"Let me handle your father. We both know his anger toward me is always short-lived."

Aaron smiled. "You are the love of his life."

"And he is second only to you. Make me proud and bring Edward's daughter to him." Guinevere let a hand linger on her son's cheek for a few moments before she turned to head down the stairs.

"Do you believe she's okay?" Aaron asked, following his mother.

"Of course. I wouldn't let you go if I wasn't certain," she said with a nod before leaving.

Aaron grabbed the last few items he'd need while his mother's words played in his head. As he hurried down the stairwell and out to the stables, he remembered the last time they'd seen Elizabeth and Victoria, before everything happened.

I can't remember why we were there, but I remember how hard Elizabeth cried when I had to leave. She reached for me and called me "hers."

Edward had even reassured her they'd come to Datten for Aaron's birthday in a few weeks.

"I doubt she'll even remember me," Aaron muttered.

"Who?" Jerome asked, holding his hand out for Aaron's bag.

"The princess."

"She might. She was almost five when she left. I have some memories from when I was that age," Megesti said.

"You can remember when you were that young?" Jerome asked.

"I'm sixty-nine. I'm not ancient." Megesti laughed and handed Jerome his bag.

The trio hurried to finish preparing the horses and then left the stable. Aaron looked up as they passed through the keep toward the Dark Forest; his mother and father were standing atop it. Guinevere waved and blew Aaron a kiss while Emmerich stoically kept his arm around his wife. Waving to his mother, Aaron disappeared into the forest.

SILENCE FILLED the inn's bar. The last overnight guest had left, and it wasn't yet time for the lunch crowd. Aaron made himself comfortable across the table from Jerome and Megesti. He surveyed the room and noticed the inn owner smiling at him. He nodded in reply. Christine had been her name. Aaron remembered names and faces. He'd talked with her and her sister, Andrea, about the challenges in their small, isolated village, and knew he'd be leaving a generous tip.

Few chairs. They don't get many patrons.

Aaron returned his attention to Jerome and Megesti. They had finished eating, and even without listening, he knew they were discussing which village to visit next. It had been three long months of this, and he wondered if it might be a lost cause. The journey was wearing on him, but he was too stubborn to give up yet.

"We're finished with St. Clement," Jerome said. "Where do you want to go next? Lorsch isn't too far, and neither is Stoney Creek, but Kirsh is more secluded, so it might be the better choice."

"Aaron? Are you paying attention?" Megesti kicked his chair, making him sit up.

"Of course I am," Aaron snapped. "I think Kirsh makes the most sense."

Megesti nodded and turned back to Jerome while Aaron began replaying the conversation with Emmerich and Edward and went over, once again, the details General Bishop provided before they left. Tomorrow would be the anniversary of Victoria's death. After fourteen years, so many rumors surrounded the disappearance of the princess.

What if we're chasing the wrong rumor?

In most of them, her grandfather had ordered the killing. Some said it was because Victoria made Edward stand up to him while others believed she was a dark sorceress and had angered the wrong sorcerer. A few thought Edward killed them both in a fit of jealous rage over one of Victoria's former lovers. Aaron knew the last one was a lie. His father would be capable of such an act, especially if drunk, but never Edward. Aaron worried about what his father would do if they came back empty-handed. Would he lose his crown for failing Edward's task? Would the kings allow them to come home, or, like a jousting run, would momentum force them to carry on regardless of the quest's futility?

Megesti slouched and fidgeted. His robes were disheveled, and his usually neat brown hair was as overgrown and snarled as the surrounding woods. The three months of traveling were wearing on him the most. Megesti rubbed his eyes before scratching his head and subsequently got his finger stuck in his hair. He pulled a stick out a moment later and dropped it on the table. Then he groaned, reached into his collar, and dropped a bunch of leaves on the table. He noticed Aaron was watching, so he pursed his lips and glared. "Why do you never have the woods in *your* clothes?"

Aaron bit back a chuckle. Megesti grumbled as he rose to shake his shirt out. A handful of twigs, leaves, and even a stone fell out of his clothes. Aaron's resolve snapped, and he laughed.

"Don't laugh at the sorcerer," Jerome said. His tone was more playful than scolding. "We haven't trained him to survive in the woods. He does better with books and a bed."

Aaron coughed to hide his laughter, but Megesti narrowed his eyes at them. Jerome sat stoic and proper despite the drudgery of their long mission. His clothes were impeccable, and even his graying red hair bent to his will and stayed in place.

"At least I don't have to worry about my father giving my job away," Megesti snapped.

Traitor.

"Not until we find your cousin," Aaron snapped back. He groaned as he pictured Wesley in his father's crown.

Jerome took it as a sign. He stood up and grabbed their bags off the unoccupied chair at their table. Aaron patted Megesti on the back, apologizing, and Megesti returned the favor. Aaron dropped a pair of the gold coins his mother had given him on the table and waved to the innkeeper. When they reached the stables behind the inn, Jerome paid the young stable boy a coin and hurried off to get their horses. Aaron leaned on the expansive stable doors and watched a boy come back with Thunder. Looking over the saddle and bags to make sure they'd be okay for the ride ahead, he pulled an apple out of his bag and held it out to his horse.

Megesti groaned as he mounted his steed. "Those were for you, not the horse."

Aaron patted Thunder before mounting him. "My apple, my call."

"That'll be enough, children." Jerome laughed as they set off for Kirsh.

The innkeeper had said they would arrive by dinner and had given them the name of the innkeepers there. Ian and Irma were purported to have some of the best food of all the surrounding towns.

I hope they have some smoked venison. I'm getting a little tired of rabbit stew.

"How long until we reach the next hamlet?" Megesti asked after a few hours of riding. Aaron and Jerome exchanged glances and sighed.

"Kirsh is close," Jerome said. "It's large enough that we should be able to buy supplies there. This deep in the Dark Forest, there aren't as many villages. People are uneasy being so close to the Ogre Mountains."

"Too many legends about monsters and wild beasts." Aaron leaned down and patted his horse. "Don't worry, Thunder. I won't let anything eat you."

"Not all legends are false, Aaron. A lot of things have been living in those mountains for centuries, and people need to be wary of them," Megesti said.

"We know for certain the wolves in this part of the forest are the most aggressive," Jerome said.

"What if the stories aren't about creatures but a sorceress?" Aaron asked.

"What do you mean?" Megesti asked.

Aaron shrugged. "We've been traveling in these woods for months and haven't found any strange creatures. What if the stories you've been hearing in the towns *are* Elizabeth? What if her powers are out of control?"

Aaron looked up into the trees and listened to the eerie quiet around them. Despite it being early afternoon, the thick springtime canopy above blocked the sun. He suddenly wondered whether they would have seen anything or anyone watching them even if they'd been looking for such things.

"I hope you're wrong, Aaron, but I have worried about what would happen if she forgot who she was and these powers manifested in her. Having them arrive when you are expecting them is hard enough, but if you don't know ..." Megesti trailed off, his thoughts somehow both unfinished and yet complete all the same. He shuddered, and his horse slowed its pace in response.

"How could she forget she's a princess? That isn't something you stop knowing," Jerome said. "It could take many months for the news of Arthur's death to reach her, especially if she's in one of the smaller secluded towns. But when it does, she'll realize she's safe. If we find her, we only need to explain that he's dead, and she'll come back with us."

"He's dead, but he couldn't give Edward any peace," Aaron said. He sped up to catch up with Jerome.

"Did you believe he would reveal anything?" Jerome asked.

"No, but I know Edward had been hoping for a deathbed confession. Arthur was a horrible king but a worse father. Even in death, he's let his son suffer unimaginable pain."

The horses' hooves clopped on the path, and the rustling leaves in the canopy above were the only other sounds as they rode on. Aaron hoped the news would reach Elizabeth so she could come out of hiding *if* she still remembered who she was. The idea haunted Aaron.

What if her powers come in and she doesn't know what they are or why she has them?

The wind picked up, sending dust and old leaves flying around them, making the horses skittish.

"Aaron. Something's coming," Megesti said.

The wind made his voice sound distant.

Jerome and Aaron halted their horses and turned back to Megesti.

"I hear nothing unusual," Jerome said.

"I felt it. The wind changed," Megesti said, dismounting. He held his hands out in front of him, and the wind rushed around him, sending his cloak and hair flying.

"The wind changes a lot here because the mountains are so close," Aaron said.

"No. This was different," Megesti said.

"Why do you always think something terrible is coming?" Jerome asked. He rolled his eyes and turned his horse around.

Aaron sighed and thrust his head toward Jerome. "We've been traveling for months. You're just tired and being paranoid."

"No. There's something here. I *feel* it."

"Megesti, what do you—?"

Aaron froze.

Megesti had gone pale.

"Jerome!" Aaron dismounted from Thunder and rushed to grab Megesti's horse. He watched Megesti's face become ashen. Hooves crunched as Jerome hurried back and leaped from his horse.

Megesti's breathing had become erratic, and his eyes were closed. An intense look overtook his face. It was one Aaron had only seen a handful of times.

He's having a vision.

"Megesti—" Aaron jumped back.

Megesti dropped to his knees, and his eyes shot open. They were pure white. He spoke slowly, in a distorted voice.

"What is lost will be found, only to then lose itself again and again.

The sea harbors the answers, but the blood reveals the truth.

Flames that don't burn will reveal a destined bond.

The wounds of the past are coming to take the future back.

His honor will be what rips them apart in the end.

Only the truly lost can save the lost.

The beast must be contained, or she'll meet her end.
A new blood oath will form from broken sons.
Your destiny is at hand, but you must fight it to win it."

Aaron threw the reins to Jerome and dashed to Megesti, grabbing him before he collapsed.

"Megesti, are you okay?" Aaron asked, helping him up.

"Aaron, did I ...?"

"Yes. You had a vision. And as usual, it made no sense."

"Not yet," Megesti said. "They always prove themselves later."

"But for now, they make no sense," Aaron said.

"What did I say?"

Aaron shrugged as he helped Megesti onto his horse. "Something about water, and fire, and destiny."

"Aaron," Jerome said. His voice was curt.

Aaron sighed and summarized Megesti's strange words back to him, using an old Warren trick Edward had taught him when he was young. Aaron had mastered it when he was ten and used it to memorize the kings' journals in order to win a disagreement with Jerome. "I don't enjoy having to fight to win my destiny. I thought destiny just happens to us."

"It seems yours doesn't. You always have been rather diffi-cult." Megesti smiled, then looked down at his hands and gasped.

"What is it?" Jerome asked.

Megesti's breaths sped up as he raised his hands. The left was glowing violet, like his Merlin line color, but the other was gold. "I was right." He looked up at Aaron with a brilliant smile.

"Right about what?" Aaron asked, moving closer to his friend again.

"She's alive, Aaron! And we're close. A son of Cassandra can't have a premonition that large without help. My father and I can combine our gifts to see something almost that large, but I can't. Not alone."

"What are you saying?" Jerome said.

"A daughter of Cassandra is somewhere nearby. The daughters of the Cassandra line inherit most of our powers. For me to have such a large vision, I need that power to come from *someone*."

"So she's here—in Kirsh?" Aaron asked.

"Get on your horses. We need to get to town as quickly as possible," Jerome said.

"Why?" Megesti asked.

Aaron laughed. "Knowing the general, he's planning to get there for dinner and buy a few rounds. Inebriated locals are more likely to let something slip."

He helped Megesti onto his horse and then mounted Thunder in one motion.

"What are we looking for?" Megesti asked.

"Any information on a family that may have taken in an orphan fourteen years ago. We can't be too obvious, or it will spook them."

"Right. Subtle," Megesti said as they sent their horses into a canter.

With luck, they would hit Kirsh before dinner.

Want to find out what happens next? Go to http://alicehanov.com for information about The Head, the Heart, and the Heir, *book one in the series, which picks up the story right from here.*

NEED MORE OF TORIAN?

If you enjoyed the book be sure to leave a review since they are a huge help to indie authors like me! They can even just be a few words that you enjoyed the book!

Join the Facebook Fan group to engage with other fans and get fun updates from Alice!

Sign up for the monthly newsletter!

Support Alice on Patreon and get early or exclusive access to things.

TORIAN TIMELINE

Sorcerers Arrive	No one Knows
Founding of Datten	year 0
Founding of Warren	50
Founding of six Southern Kingdoms	50-100
Merlock & Victoria arrive in Datten	1469
Megesti is born	1483
Arthur of Warren is born	1484
Gryphon is born	1488
Emmerich of Datten is born	1503
Edward of Warren is born	1510
King Emmerich is crowned King of Datten	1516
Prince Daniel of Datten is born	1522
Prince Aaron of Datten is born	1530
Princess Elizabeth of Warren (Alex) is born	1533
Princess Elizabeth vanishes	
Princess Victoria is murdered	
Prince Daniel is killed	1538
Princess Alex returns to Warren	1552

A Note from the Author

When I started writing this series, I was intending to write a YA epic fantasy, but my characters had other ideas.

The themes and tropes that are developing as the story caries on, especially book 3 and on are of a much more adult level than originally expected. So in order to be true to the characters and meet reader expectations I'm aging everyone up 2 years.

So if you read this before March 15, 2024 the characters would have been younger than they are in this edition. A detailed breakdown is on my website if you need to visually see what happened.

Thank you for your understanding.

PRONUNCIATION GUIDE

Bernhard: Burn-hart
Betruger: Beh-true-grrrr
Datten: Day-ten
Ferflucs: Fair-f-looks
Kirsh: K-ear-sh
Kruft: K-ruff-t
Merlock: Mer-lock
Nial: N-aisle
Ogre: O-grah
Oreean: Or-ian
Rassgat: Ras-gat
Torian: Tore-ian
Warren: War-en

KINGDOMS
DATTEN

Motto: Honor above All

Royal Family
King Emmerich (1503–)
Queen Guinevere (1504–)
Dead Prince Daniel (1521–1538)
Prince Aaron (1530–)

House of Wafner
Jerome (General of Datten) and dead Lady Gwendalin
Seven children: Patrick (Stefan), Jessica, dead Ryan, Arthur, Samuel, Olivia, and David

House of Merlock
Merlock: royal sorcerer and king's advisor
Megesti: sorcerer apprentice and Merlock's son

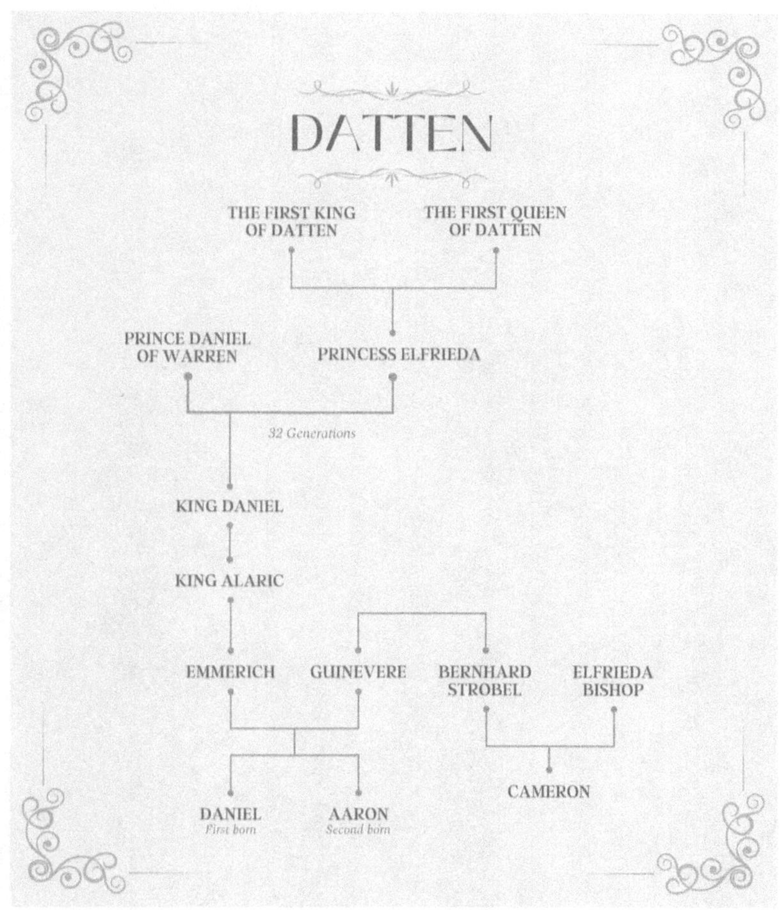

DATTEN
THE FIRST KING OF DATTEN
THE FIRST QUEEN OF DATTEN
PRINCE DANIEL OF WARREN
PRINCESS ELFRIEDA
32 Generations
KING DANIEL
KING ALARIC
EMMERICH
GUINEVERE
BERNHARD STROBEL
ELFRIEDA BISHOP
CAMERON
DANIEL
First born
AARON
Second born

KINGDOMS
WARREN

Motto: Prosperity through Courage

Royal Family
King Edward (1509–)
Dead Princess Victoria (1451–1538)
Princess Elizabeth aka Alex (1533–)

House of Nial
Randal (General of Warren) and Lady Judith
Three daughters: Abigail, Diana, and Edith

House of Bishop
Matthew (retired general) and Lady Lillian
Three sons: Marco, Aiden, and Julius

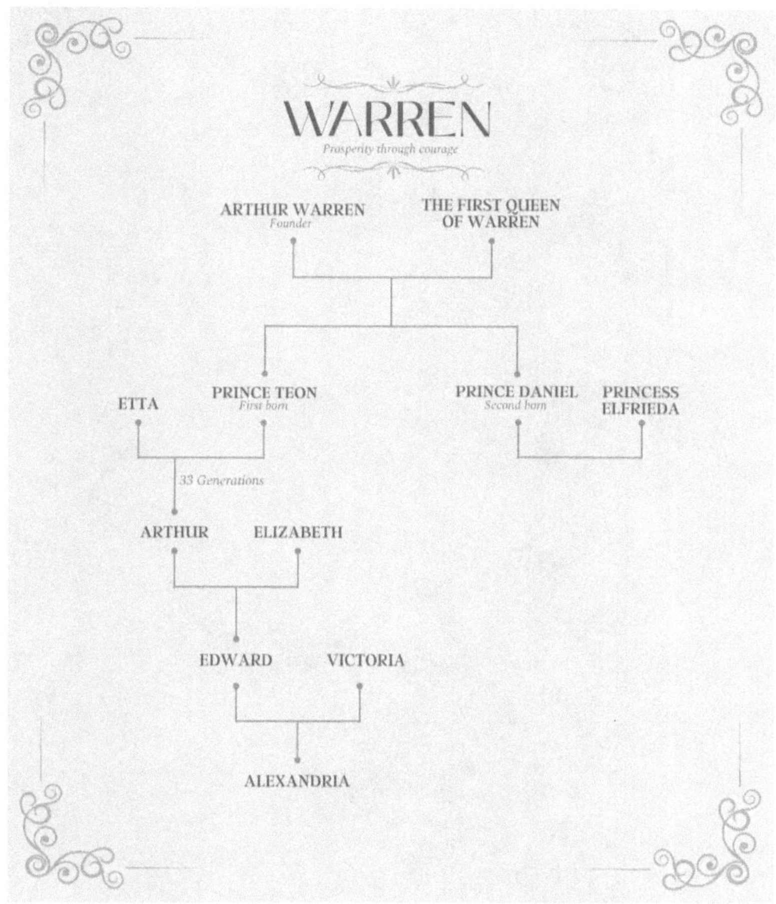
WARREN
Prosperity through courage
ARTHUR WARREN
Founder
THE FIRST QUEEN
OF WARREN
PRINCE TEON
First born
PRINCE DANIEL
Second born
PRINCESS
ELFRIEDA
ETTA
33 Generations
ARTHUR
ELIZABETH
EDWARD
VICTORIA
ALEXANDRIA

KINGDOMS

BETRUGER

Motto: Legacy Never Dies

Royal Family
King Harold (1525–)

House of Macht
Bruno (Head Guard of Betruger)

SORCERERS OF TORIAN

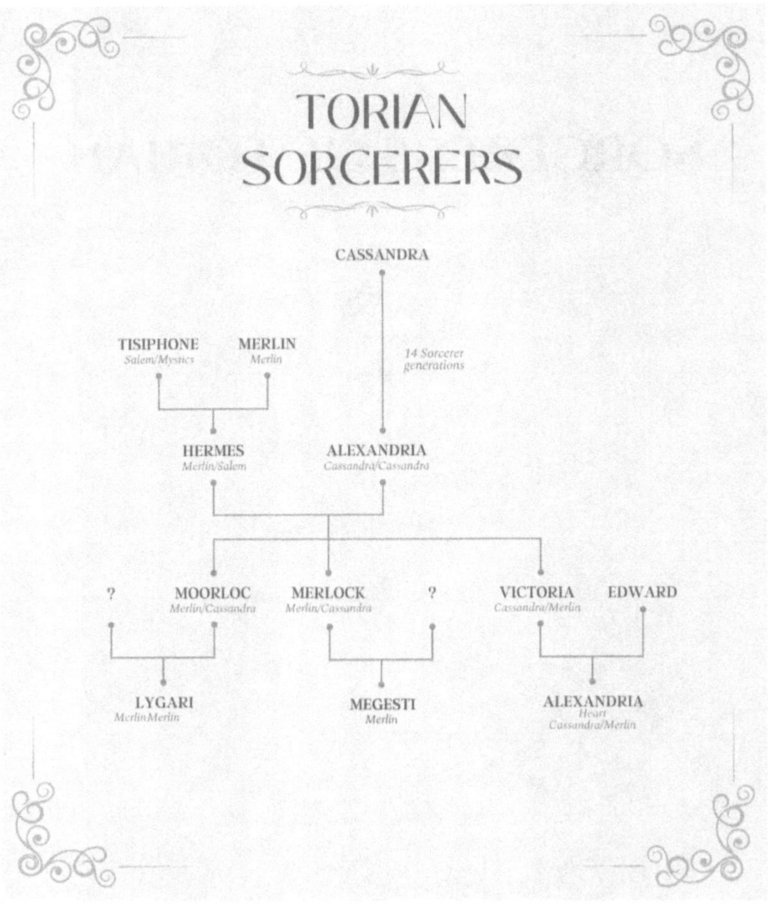
TORIAN
SORCERERS
CASSANDRA
TISIPHONE
Salem/Mystics
MERLIN
Merlin
14 Sorcerer
generations
HERMES
Merlin/Salem
ALEXANDRIA
Cassandra/Cassandra
?
MOORLOC
Merlin/Cassandra
MERLOCK
Merlin/Cassandra
?
VICTORIA
Cassandra/Merlin
EDWARD
LYGARI
Merlin Merlin
MEGESTI
Merlin
ALEXANDRIA
Heart
Cassandra/Merlin

ARES

- orange
- chaos and violence

CASSANDRA

- gold
- healing and premonitions

CELTICS

- light green
- plants and peace

HADES

- grey
- death related

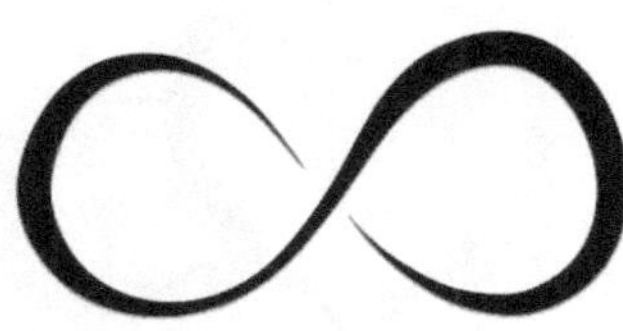

MERLIN

- violet
- varies

MIRE

- brown
- earth powers

Mystics

- royal blue
- mind control

Poseidon

- dark blue
- water and weather

Salem

- maroon
- fire and explosions

Tiere

- dark green
- animal powers

Head

- one of two strongest born in a generation
- logic ruled

Heart

- other strongest born in a generation
- emotional ruled

PRONUNCIATION GUIDE

Ares: Air-ease

Bernhard: Burn-hart

Betruger: Beh-True-Grrrr

Cassandra: Cas-an-draw

Celtic: Kel-tick

Datten: Day-ten

Ferflucs: Fair-f-looks

Hades: Hay-dees

Lygari: Le-garh-ee

Kirsh: K-ear-sh

Kruft: K-ruff-t

Merlin: Mer-lin

Merlock: Mer-lock

Mire: Mirr-ah

Moorloc: More-lock

Mystics: Myst-ics

Nial: N-aisle

Ogre: O-grah

Oreean: Or-ian

Poseidon: Poe-sigh-done

Rassgat: Ras-gat

Salem: Say-lem

Tiere: Teer-rah

Torian: Tore-Ian

Warren: War-en

GLOSSARY

Betrayer: term used for a sorcerer who tries to kill or severely wound their own family. Appears as three *x*'s stacked on top of each other on the left inner forearm.

Bond marks: a mark that a mated pair of sorcerers share. Each is unique, made up of their line marks, and can appear on the back of either shoulder or neck.

Hexa: sorcerer grandmother.

Hexen: sorcerer grandfather.

Line marks: images used to show the ten sorcerer lines.

Magician: insult that implies a person has no power as all human "magicians" were frauds.

Pearls: magical spheres that show the past (clear), present (white), and future (black).

Returned one: a sorcerer who dies but is brought back.

Sorcerer line: also known as a line, this is the legacy of sorcerers born from a founding sorcerer. For example, the line of Merlin includes all Merlin sorcerers born from him with Merlin powers.

Sorcerer awakening: a time in a sorcerer's life when they go through puberty and subsequently receive their powers and learn which line they are.

Sorcerer: sorcerer who identifies as male.

Sorceress: sorcerer who identifies as female.

Sorcerous: sorcerer who identifies as neither male nor female, nonbinary.

Titan: strongest sorcerer of a particular line.

Usurper: a special sorcerer born every two or three generations who can borrow or siphon the power of sorcerers around them. Only one can ever be alive at a time.

Witch: insult that implies a person has no power as all human "witches" were frauds.

SERIES LINKS

The Spare Who Became the Heir and Other Stories

The Head, the Heart, and the Heir

Broken Sons

The Heir Rises

The Last True Heirs

Book 5 - coming late 2024

Book 6 - coming 2025

Book 7 - coming 2025

Extended Omnibus Kickstarter

Volume 1 - May 2024

Volume 2 - February 2025

Volume 3 - November 2025

ACKNOWLEDGMENTS

This book came together after the novel was written as a way for me to share the details of the characters' lives with my friends and followers. I ended up turning it into this book because I thought everyone should be able to enjoy knowing Alex, Aaron, and all their friends on a deeper level.

First and foremost, I have to thank my husband, Steve, and my children, Lillian, Katrina, and Zack. They have learned to leave mommy alone when she writes and try not to disturb my writing time, and I cannot thank them enough for that. Steve makes my writing a priority even on days where I don't think I should, and it's because of his dedication that I can write as much as I do.

To my mom, Elke, and stepdad, Al, I want to say thank you for letting me be as weird and crazy as I wanted to be all through high school and teaching me that being different is great.

To my Oma Elfieda in Germany, I want to thank you for giving me a typewriter when I visited in the summer when I was seven. You allowed me to write all the stories in my head and helped to start me on this journey.

To my amazing online BookTok and Bookstagram friends, thank you for bringing a smile to my face and giving me a safe place to vent and talk books and cry when I needed. A special thank you to Brittany N., Codi E., Natalie, Santi, and Mia.

To my fantastic author friends I found online—you are

shining lights in my dark days. You understand the pain and loneliness that comes with writing and also laugh and share stories about the craziest things we have had to google! Nikki, Tiffany, Amanda, Sonja, Penelope, Ruby, Rosalyn, Laura, Bekah, Jillian, Lynn, and countless more—you all make writing so much more enjoyable!

I also want to thank my ARC readers and my street team for taking a chance on my story and helping to get my book out there!

Along with you all, I must thank my alpha readers, Andrea Hernandez and Christine Hutton. You two have listened to all my crazy ideas, overzealous excitement, and always wanted to hear more. Thank you for your enthusiasm, encouragement, and your love for my characters, my world, and my story.

Thank you to my brilliant artists who helped my line marks and characters come to life! Casey (of RallyBirdBrand), your work is fantastic, and your series and sorcerer marks are just perfect! I love that I got to use them as chapter headings too. Hoang Tejieng, your renderings of my characters helped bring them to life for me, and I love having them around to help inspire me.

To my author critique group—Stephanie Joyce and Amanda Terry Hamm. You two understand me in a way that is shocking, and despite my crazy energetic antics, you stick around. I appreciate you more than I could ever say, so instead, I will continue to mail you random bookmarks, chocolate, and other randomness because together we WILL conquer the world.

To my photographer, Brittany Nosal—I have never had so much fun on a photo shoot, and I cannot thank you enough for helping bring the true me out in my photos. You gave me photos that are not only professional enough for my work but also still have a whimsical air about them.

I also want to take a moment to thank the team of Intrepid Literary.

Lauren, you are the coolest CEO I have ever met. Every time we have a meeting, I'm so excited, and it just makes my day. Thank you for being so amazing and helping me achieve my dream and also for having the same energy and excitement for my books as I do.

Shannon, you are so amazing. I can't thank you enough for helping keep all my work on track and making sure we don't miss anything!

Sam, my amazing developmental editor, thank you for being as in love with my world as I am. I love working with you, and I look forward to your thoughts on future books!

Brian, thank you for helping make my words flow so that I get my point across in the most concise way possible. Thank you for saving my readers from my superfluous and redundant verbosity.

Jackie, you are a grand grammar guru! You made sure people could breathe when they read my work and that all my capitals and their/they're/theres were in the right place!

To my cover designers, Alan and Ian—I cannot thank you enough for my gorgeous cover! Thank you for working with me and helping this cover fit with the first but not take away from what will be my proper series covers!

S. E.—You are not just my senior editor but my coach, my freak-out person, and my books' big sibling. Talking with you is like talking to an older sibling; they know more than me and make sure I get told what I need to know kindly so I can make things better, but they'll celebrate every achievement with me in the best way possible. Thank you! I look forward to working with you on many more books! Lauren—you can't take S. E. away from me!

Lastly, I want to thank all the amazing fantasy authors

whose work helped me find a safe place to go to when I needed to escape the cold world—from Mary Shelley to J. R. R. Tolkien to Sarah J. Maas and Holly Black as well as Homer and the scholars of Greek mythology who gave me the inspiration for so much of this world. Thank you for changing my life!

About the Author

Photo by Brittany Jean Photography

Alice Hanov was born in Germany and then raised on Pelee Island in the middle of one of the Great Lakes, spending her days imagining grand adventures in the woods around the island. She has never stopped writing and has a degree in rhetoric and professional writing from the University of Waterloo. Alice lives in Ontario with her hubby and three kids, various pets, and many, many books. You can visit her online at alicehanov.com.

9 781778 047640